OVER A CUP OF TEA

"Flavours, Colours and Taste"
(A Collection of Short Stories)

By Anagh Madhavan

First Published in July 2021
ISBN: 978-93-5472-435-0

BLUEROSE PUBLISHERS
www.bluerosepublishers.com
info@bluerosepublishers.com
+91 8882 898 898
Distributed by: BlueRose, Amazon, Flipkart, Shopclues

Homage

To my parents late Shri. E.U. Madhavan & late Smt Ambika Madhavan.
"You will be with me until the very end."

"This book is gifted to my wife Shobha and grandchild Sai"

Preface

Dear Readers,

Tea has many flavours, colours, and taste, same as we humans.

Our world consists of different countries, people, and cultures. People from politics, academics, media, films and TV, students, the young and the old with different qualities, characters, attitudes, all come together 'Over a cup of tea.'

Tea proves its credentials, it brings its best form and serves various purpose all around the world, attains different forms, names, colours, flavours, and taste, but at the same time retains the basic qualities. It is powered and activates the mood of every one.

The green tea, black tea, masala tea, ginger tea, lemon tea, sugarless tea and various other forms, where tea remains a catalyst.

Every country, region, city, town and village have a different style of preparing tea. Habits are formed around a bed tea or a morning tea which goes with a newspaper on the breakfast table.

People while travelling, in a meeting, political gathering, celebrations, parties and get together prefer to have their talks & mood to go with a cup of tea. It has assumed an important stature and has greatly influenced our daily life. We find a tea stall, in every street, at bus stops, highways, railway stations, airports, offices, restaurants, hotels and all around us.

Where ever we go we will find a tea stall. At certain places it is costly and sometimes unaffordable. It has a wonderful combination of colours and flavours.

The stories in the forthcoming pages are similar to tea with different flavours, colours and taste.

Sincere thanks to my son Shreenath,my friend Malvika Tiwary for helping me with editing, my nephew Hari Ajith for the layout and cover design, my brother Anil for overall assistance in bringing out this book.

Enjoy reading one sip at a time, 'over a cup of tea.'

Anagh Madhavan.

Prelude

The Author's inspiration and interest is evidenced in his compilation of short stories in here. He has thrown hopes of amelioration of mankind with the moral, expressed at the end of every story, and sinks into a very well articulated style of expressing clearly and effectively, disguising the same under the soft titles and contempt for visionary philosophies in the form of short stories to come out with things one could relate to.

I have great pleasure in writing a prelude for this book "Over a Cup of Tea" (A Collection of Short Stories) compiled by my brother and edited by his son Shreenath in his own lucid style in English now ready for printing.

It is really a marvellous tribute to our parents. Whereby life is illustrated through various stories for easy understanding.

In as much as I know my brother, he has developed language skills through collaborative and interactive tasks around literary texts. This has helped him to develop a lifelong habit of reading. Managing the reading habit and building a reading profile has trained his mind to think logically and also taught him to have an open mind.

His determination to develop a strong reading habit and expression of his thoughts in a lucid manner has provided him abundant opportunities to use language in meaningful and real-life contexts. This has motivated him to bring out this book for all of us to read and be known to various phases of life and psychology of people which exist in certain cross section of people in the neighbourhood.

He dedicates this book to his beloved wife and grandchild, amply justifying the profound love he has for his family as he still works to keep them happy braving all odds and takes life in his stride with all the ease he can at a remarkable age of 72. And therefore it will be worthwhile to spend some time to read this book definitely over a cup of tea as the author suggests.

Anil Madhavan

OVER A CUP OF TEA

"Flavours, Colours and Taste"
(A Collection of Short Stories)

Contents. Pg Pg

Stories.

1. Inspiring Seashore.

I could hear the distant splash of the sea. The sea was silent, but vibrant. It was low tide. I could walk some distance into the sea's territory as the sea distanced itself from the shore, exposing the slippery rocks. I occupied the deserted territory on the sea shore for a few hours, or rather should I say that the kind hearted sea allowed me to get closer to its core?

One thing is for sure, nothing is permanent.

The sea is tolerant and quiet today, and this gives me more breathing space and time. The fishermen's boats anchored during the high tide are now humbled, stagnant and resting on tiny rocks, waiting to return to its adventure.

Some people are busy collecting pebbles and seashells, while some are not even bothered to look at the wealth brought to the shores; for some, it is priceless and for some it is worthless.

Some people come here to breath fresh air, admire nature and exercise through morning walks, jogging and yoga. Some are loners, depressed and frustrated. Then there are the regular fishermen who set their nets during the low tide and wait for the high tide to return with a good catch.

Life is a cycle with high and low tides, ups and downs, where we see our own shadows turning taller and shorter. You cannot measure your shadows. All you have to do is to tide over the situations yourself. Nobody can share your suffering; even Christ had to bear his own cross.

There, at a distance, I can see a lighthouse. It serves as a saviour for the boats and ships, guiding them to the right path amidst darkness.

The sea inspires us and gives us valuable guidelines on the philosophy of life. Going by what the sea offers, I am sure no one ever goes back empty handed.

"Never give up hope. Hope against hope is the key."

2. Barbie Doll.

He used to always look at the gift shop from outside; he knew if he gets close to the glass door they will drive him out. He counted the money opening his fist; he knew it wasn't enough to buy that beautiful Barbie doll for which his little sister was crying.

He works at a tea stall, his parents were casual labourers. It has been two years of hard labour at the tea stall. His day comprised of a 12 hour work schedule starting from 7:00 am in the morning which extended up to 7:00 pm in the evening. His duties included cleaning the glasses and kettles, arranging the cups and saucer and filling gigantic water tubs with water. He had to rush towards the always-in-a-hurry municipal water tanker and store the water in large carboys, load them into a hand cart and pull it till his workstation. All this work fetched him Rs. 20 a day.

Our hero used to get one rupee for all his hard work and the rest was kept by his father. At a tender age of 10, when other kids were busy with their gully cricket he was busy playing the role of a bread winner for his family.

He was enterprising, at times customers at the tea stall used to tip him with loose change when ever he got them chewing tobacco or a cigarette from the pan shop near by. He used to hand all the money to the owner of the tea stall as his savings.

The shop was a customary stop for me for my daily dose of tea. I was what you call a 'regular' at the shop. Over a period of time I grew fond of the kid, sometimes I felt pity for the boy. He used to always greet me with a smile and a glass of water. Almost everyday I would be the first customer at their tea stall. The boy's name was Laxman, I used to distort his name and call him Lacchu out of affection.

The owner of the tea stall was a kind man, sometimes when it wasn't busy at the stall he would get some snacks and give it to Laxman. Laxman had never seen the gate of a school. I feel pity for him. Many a times the thought of meeting his parents and convincing them to put him in a school crossed my mind. I thought I should suggest them to enroll him in a government run school which would not be a burden to them, as they don't have to pay any fees there.

One day I asked Lachhu,"will you take me to your parents; I would like to meet them."

Lachhu agreed and after his working hours I accompanied him to his home. He took me to a slum where his father and mother had just reached home. His little sister was very loving and smart; she hugged Lachhu and both of them dashed out to play with the other kids from the locality.

There were several of them; I was sure none of them saw the face of a school. Most of them irrespective of their age were working to contribute to the family income or for one single meal a day. Lachhu's mother returned with some oil, masala, some rice and dal from the nearby shop. I asked them "Do you buy these items on a daily basis? Don't you eat vegetables?" Lachhu's father replied that it is a struggle to get one square meal for the family even after pooling in all the three wages.

I have read a lot about poverty, about slums and the hardships, but this is the first time I encountered it first hand. The conditions there are very pathetic, it's a living hell. How can we claim we are an independent developing nation? Its futile to even ask them to send their children to school without understanding their fundamental problem; hunger superseded everything. I was very much disturbed after visiting Laxman's home that I did not take my dinner. My son who is studying in the 5th standard came running to me, "Papa did you bring the colour pencil for me?" I was lost in thoughts, I wasn't listening to him, and in my mind I was comparing the disparity that existed in our society. What could be done to help those unfortunate kids?

Next day I asked my son to give away some of his toys. He was not ready to part with any of them. I did not scold him, instead, I thought of taking him to meet Laxman. As it is he was daily playing with the society kids, today I told him that for a change I was taking him to a new place and that over there he would make new friends.

Sunanda, my wife protested when I told her that I am taking Rahul to the slum children. I kept my calm and asked her to join us, "if you don't come you will never have an idea what you missed in life".

Sunanda and myself with our son Rahul left on our bike towards the slum. I had also asked the tea stall owner to meet me at Lacchu's place. My son was over anxious, he knew when Papa was making a plan to take him somewhere, it would be a wonderful place. I was not sure how they would react but right now they are with me.

Rahul had taken along with him some of his toys in a bag to play with the new friends.

He was excited; he was just like any of today's kids, already an expert in playing mobile games. He used to beat me hands down when ever we played games on the computer. He had everything at home; his routine for the week was preset. Every Tuesday he would be at the skating club, Saturdays were reserved for swimming; rest of the Days park was the place where he would sweat it out. Sunday outing with parents had become a ritual.

Sunanda was clue less, all she knew was that I was taking our son to the slums, so she decided to tag herself along with us. Her idea of the slum was that it was where children from well to do families would pick up dirty language and wrong habits, but at the same time I knew she was also a lady filled with compassion. All this while in my mind only one thing was going on, as to what could be done about it, this was the stark reality in our face. The government should do something for these kids, we as individuals have limitations.

We reached the slum and the entire population there gathered around us as if we are from planet Mars. It was a surprise for them to see us there. They had a folding cot which they spread out and offered us to sit and they stood there with folded hands. The tea stall owner also arrived. The slum wasn't strange to him. He too once lived there; only a few years back he shifted to a better locality.

The slum children gathered around Rahul. The only difference between Rahul and them was that while he was wearing branded clothes, most of the kids were shirtless, their shorts were dirty but they seemed to be comfortable in it.

Rahul took out his toys and the kids started getting around him like a honey bee attracting the rest of its folks. It made me wonder if the words unhygienic or foul mouth were words meant only for elders and that children are guarded from these mindset issues. There we saw a set of parents even cautioning their kids to stay away, perhaps in fear as to what would happen if their child broke a toy.

"Look Sunanda, this is the difference, they will not advance unless given permission, they are poor but equally intelligent, they are poor but they know they should not cross the line, they are deprived but they don't feel jealous of what we have, they have self respect, have you noticed that no one has uttered a single bad word, look at the discipline they are showing, all of them are standing in a straight line. Don't you think that it's our duty to try and make some difference in their lives, bring smiles on their face even for some time wouldn't it be great?" She nodded in approval.

Children are masters at breaking ice, they don't take the time we grown ups take to mingle. Rahul was all down and dirty with the kids. Meanwhile Lacchu approached the tea stall owner and asked for the money he had been depositing all this while. The owner wasn't carrying all that cash with him. Lacchu asked for whatever was with him at the time. He collected the money and came to me. Lachhu opened his fist, offered me the money and said "Sir I was collecting this money only to buy a Barbie doll for my little sister; who once cried desperately outside the shop. If it is less, I will pay you later, but could you please give me that Barbie doll? Look at my sister she has her eyes fixed on it".

On hearing this Sunanda broke down, tears rolled out from her eyes. She hugged Lacchu and his sister and offered Rahul's toys to all the kids present there.

This visit to the slum had changed Rahul; suddenly my little boy had matured. Rahul did not oppose. He had learnt the most important lesson of life. He understood the joy of giving. The lessons he learned that day was of immense value. He thanked us for taking him there.

We regularly go for family outings and trips, but this trip was far more rewarding and life changing for us. Till the time we reached home none of us talked to each other, the silence was that of contemplation.

Long after we left there was still a little girl cuddling up with her new priced possession, her new BARBIE DOLL.

"The joy of Sharing time with the less fortunate."

3. Blood is thicker.

The old man was unable to speak. He somehow managed to reach the 'Holy old age home'. The warden offered a chair and made him comfortable and then took him to the manager Smt. Simran.

The manager gave a patient hearing. This old man Keshav Rao, is a retired officer from a private company. He lost his wife couple of years back; there after he was put up with his son. He is in his eighties, he had very faint vision due to diabetes and around five years back he had implanted a pace maker due to his skipped heart beat.

Simran, the manager was filling out the form of Keshav Rao. She asked him "Uncle in this particular column you have to provide a contact number and address of a close relative, so that we can inform them incase of an emergency".

Keshav Rao did not expect this question. He hesitated and took a deep breath which conveyed his reluctance. He asked "Can we not skip this column?" She replied with firmness "No uncle; it is a legal formality, in case of any eventuality we can inform the concerned people".

"I am a surplus my dear! Even my grandchildren neglect me. There is constant quarrel in the house between my son and my daughter in law on account of me. She even tried to send me off to some Ashram while my son was abroad on official work. I resisted, but how long can I withstand this pain of knowing that im a burden to my own child. That is why I am here.'

"Every one coming here has a story, and its almost similar. People have lost their patience and tolerance. Our trustees are taking care of all the expenses, giving particular attention to the health and hygene of inmates. We have donors from all over the world, and there is hope as long as such people are there.

You may deposit any documents or valuables with us with a contact list or a nominee to claim in case of any eventuality".

Keshav Rao pulled out a large sealed envelope from his suitcase, he gave her his son's address and phone number. "After my demise you may inform him or post it to his address".

Keshav Rao was very comfortable in the new environment, in the company of new friends. The staff was very lively and took care of them all with utmost care.

A year passed and he hardly realised. During this time no one contacted him. Not even his son. At times he would be lost in thoughts and felt lonely, but his mates would always cheer him up.

When alone, Keshav Rao asked only one question to himself and God, "What for am I alive!" He never got an answer.

It so happened that one morning, he did not wake up, he passed away in his sleep. All inmates gathered to pay their respect to their friend and were fixing their turns themselves, as who will be the next. They were living for the sake of living, but none of them wished to stretch any further. This is a tragedy of this century.

There were no response to the telephone calls made to his son. After waiting for three days they performed the last rites. Keshav Rao immersed and merged in to mother earth, his body was reduced to ashes, that is the ultimate truth of life.

Simaran was holding the envelope, thinking what to do with it. Should she open and look for the contents to get some clue? Just then a man in his sixties entered asking for Keshav Rao. "I am his son, I was away, and I wish to seek forgiveness of my father who is put up here. Please allow me to meet him". His eyes were filled with tears, his voice choked.

"For almost one and a half years you never bothered to find out in what condition he is, you never visited him even once during this period. We tried to contact you to inform that your father has left this world forever. He left this envelope for you. We were thinking what to do with it. Good that you have come, we are deeply relieved'.

Knowing that his beloved father is no more in this world, he was unconsolably weeping. He was praying for forgiveness. The old inmates of his father consoled him and gave him courage to face the situation.

Deeply disturbed and disappointed he left for home that day, only to return next day early in the morning to meet Simran with the opened envelope.

"Madam I have no right to claim this, it is the last savings of his life. In spite of all the sufferings, hardships, he was still thinking about me. I wish to donate the entire sum to your 'Holy old age home'. Let it be a parting gift from my father. God bless you for looking after the abandoned old people". He handed over the envelope and left the place.

It is difficult to understand life and people. Keshav Rao could not take the decision to donate the money, it shows how much he loved his son. In spite of all the miseries and sorrows imposed by the family members and though the 'Holy old age home' was meeting all their requirements, why was he still unable to donate with an open mind? Why did he hold it back and give it to the same people who did not bother to look after him?

It is a mystery to understand the human mind. They can never part away with their possessions till the end. Surely 'Blood is thicker than water.'

4. Destiny in the Coffin.

Yesterday I died. When the evening sun spread its colours over the prevailing blue sky, just as the scene was changing on this side of the earth, inching towards darkness silently, that night I died.

In a few moments I was awakened. I was travelling through the clouds and thousands of stars at lightening speed. I crossed the rough sea overriding the rising waves, just for a few moments.

When I gained consciousness, I was in the city police lock up. "You were the first person to cry on receiving the news of my death, all others just disowned me. I was a failure on this earth, in a society with no ethics and values".

This happened yesterday, when Inspector Vikram arrested me with gold bars worth crores. He had more sympathy rather than anger while arresting me.

When I go down the memorey lane during my school days, I remember Vikram my class mate was good in sports but he always neglected studies. When I used to come first in the class Vikram used to say, "You have a bright future; but people like me are a burden to this world". The same Vikram arrested me. He is an officer enforcing law and order, and I am a criminal breaking rules and regulations.

I hope you forgive me Shanti. After my graduation when I failed to get a job; repeatedly after every attempt, when I was frustrated and disappointed and when I returned home tired, you always used to encourage me. I still hear your words, "very soon you will get a job, you are there in my daily prayers".

Those who studied with me are all well settled in life, holding good jobs and respectable position, why only me...!!

I was deliberately reaching late at night to avoid meeting neighbours. One day when I reached home, my mom told me "Your food is kept on the table", "No mom I have no appetite today". My dad vented his feelings as if to no one, "We mortgaged this house to meet the college fees, but see what is the gain".

There were plenty of expectations from me. I was silently listening to all these and spending sleepless nights. I desperately tried to push back those melancholic thoughts in the darkness. At times I felt like running away from all these, but how can I abandon my old parents.

It was during this period I met Iqbal Quereshi, who was my classmate. He was doing business in Gulf. When we met he was shocked that I was struggling for a job.

"I will try to help you get a job". How happy I was to hear those wonderful words. It gave me a ray of hope.

When we met near the temple you told me, "I offered special prayer for you to get a suitable job". I could read from those beautiful eyes, your innocence, your ignorance of this cruel world, the world of sorrows and miseries.

One late night when I returned home, my mom was seriously sick and coughing heavily. Dad was very much desperate and helpless. He told me, "I do not have any money with me to take her to a doctor". Tired and exhausted I came out of the house. I was back with a doctor, it stunned me when he told she is starving. The doctor said she needs proper food and to take her to a good hospital and get her treated.

I cried that day, first time in my life. I sold the parker pen that I won in an essay competition and borrowed some money from Iqbal Quereshi. One day Iqbal Quereshi told me the secret of generating wealth. 'Smuggling!!' A quick shiver passed through my entire body. I looked into his eyes and yelled, "You people have sold the nation, destroyed the high human values, now you want to destroy me?". He just gave me a sarcastic smile and went away.

At night I could hear my mom coughing uncontrollably. I felt so helpless. My parents sacrificed everything for me throughout their life, and I stood watching them die helplessly. Only once my dad uttered, "You just watch everything silently". My mom said, "My sickness is such that no one can do anything, not even God". Dad in a depressive tone commented, "At least we can claim our son is there to see us die".

It was a great blow, I could not take it, I hated myself. Why I am only gifted with sorrow, grief, pain and darkness all around.

Behind these iron bars, when I go down the memory lane, I remember those days when teachers used to give me as an example to other students,"You must learn from him, he is a role model for all of you".

I met Iqbal Quereshi and told him I am willing to do business with him. I could sense that he did not trust me completely.

'This is the truth.'

Yesterday I was caught red-handed by Inspector Vikram. I died instantly. Here I am in this prison cell as a changed man. I failed to hold on to the high values which I preached so long, I got derailed from the moral path at the weakest moment of my life.

I could hear the rhythm of systematic drill carried out by the guards outside the prison. They are people enforcing law and order in the society.

"Never imagine a life without ethics and values."

5. A Mother's Agony

Shabana was pregnant, her boyfriend deserted her. She was down and depressed, she left the hostel, gave up her studies, she never wanted to go home as she will never be able to face her parents.

She travelled to a different destination towards east, landed at a catholic church at Kolkatta, where the church was also running an orphanage home.

Shabana prayed to the mother superior, "Let me give birth to my child, I can't kill my child , let my child see this world, Let the whole world blame me. I made a terrible mistake. Please forgive me mother", she fainted and collapsed there.

On gaining consciousness she repeated the same thing, "Please let me stay here till I give birth to my child, there after I will go away".

Mother Superior allowed her to stay there, but she insisted to know how, where and with whom she was involved.

Shabana was all the time worried, how she will manage after the delivery, how she will look after the child, how she will carry the child. She has to move out from this place. If her community comes to know about this, they will object her stay here and the church administration will also face trouble. She decided in her mind; soon after the delivery she will move out leaving the child in their care. She will come back and claim later on when she is capable of taking care of her child.

After six months Shabana delivered a cute little baby girl. she was darling of all the sisters of the chapel.

A month after the delivery Shabana left the church and the orphanage home leaving a note for mother superior to take care of her child.

There were nearly twenty children of different age groups, abandoned by such parents, leaving them at their door steps. People do not understand the seriousness of their acts and forget everything for a moment's lust and pleasure.

One evening a couple arrived at the orphanage run by the church. They expressed their desire to adopt a child.They went through the album and set their eyes on this particular child of Shabana. She was only one month old.

The sisters suggested and insisted to go for a grown up child, as she is only one month old, moving out at this stage will have problems, as she is also deprived of mother's milk.

Manisha asked permission to see the child, she was very happy of her selection as she was a cute little doll. The child suddenly started crying, the sisters tried to calm her. Another sister explained to Manisha that this was the problem adopting an infant at this tender age. It will be very challenging to nurse and raise the child. Manisha was not at all listening to the sister, she walked towards the sister who was trying to calm the child. Manisha took the child in her arms, pressed her close to her heart. She longed for this moment. Tears rolled out of her eyes, the child stopped crying instantly. It was magic! All eyes glued on her, and lost in the union of a mother and child.

The orphanage had no hesitation to hand over the child to these parents as they were pleased that the infant bonded with the mother.

They told them the child was christened a few days ago as 'Angelina.'

Manisha and Malay completed the formalities, took the child with them and proceeded to Singapore where Malay was employed.

After three years, Shabana, who was then married in her own community returned to the church to see and claim her child. She wanted to adopt her own child, she had only told her husband that she wanted to adopt a child as she is getting bored all alone in the house.

Mother superior was furious, but controlled her anger, she spoke to her at length, and assured her child was safe and in good care of decent and well to do people.

Shabana was disappointed but was helpless, as she was once obliged by the orphanage, it was her fault she left abruptly leaving her child there, she understood she has no right over her claim. She can not reveal this to her husband; she has to live with it.

Manisha was busy all the time looking after her child that she hardly gave any attention to Malay. He too was very fond of Angelina.

Manisha will hold the baby close to her; she liked the smell of the tiny little child.

Soon Angelina grew up under the care of her parents, with all luxuries and comforts of life, she finished her graduation and started working in a private firm as a trainee. For Manisha she was still a little girl: she would start worrying if she came late from office. The moment she comes from office she tries to make her comfortable and feed her.

One day somehow Angelina came to know that, she is the adopted child of Manisha and Malay. This disturbed her. She could no more be with her parents as before. She never had the courage to ask this to either Manisha or Malay.

Manisha observed there is something that was bothering Angelina.

One more question bothered Manisha constantly, her motherhood was telling her, some day she will have to face questions from Angelina!, she and Malay will have to disclose the facts at the time of her marriage, and how to deal with such a situation worried her. This disturbed both Manisha and Malay.

Life has many twists; nobody can claim they do not have worries and sufferings.

One day Angelina mustered all her courage and asked Malay about the truth.

Malay took her for a long drive and told everything about her past. He told her they were to reveal this at an appropriate time.

It was a great relief for both Malay and Angelina.

Manisha was getting restless and worried; she could make out the change of attitude in Angelina for the past couple of days. Her doubts were strong when Malay and Angelina went out under some shopping excuse. She was very much worried as what must be the matter, unknowingly tears rolled from her eyes, she started crying. Just then the door bell rang. She ran and opened the door. She was still crying uncontrollably. She took Angelina in her arms the same way she took her twenty years back. She hugged her and kissed her. Both Manisha and Angelina were crying. She took her mother's face between her palms, and told her "I love you mamma, I will stay with you forever, I will never be able to repay what you have done for me, I love you both".

It was a great moment in their life .The bonds of love was stronger now.

Relatioships are built on mutual understanding, respect for each other, by love and above all faith in God.

6. Lost and found.

Shivani was waiting for her turn for the second round of her interview for the job of a secretary. She wanted this job desperately as they were living in a joint family. She lost her father who worked as an artisan in a private firm. After the demise of her father it was becoming more and more difficult for her mother and herself to continue in the joint family.

In the second round of interview, she found there were three officials, who made her comfortable for the session. She replied all the questions directed to her in a very professional manner.

Among the three, there was an elderly official Gupta, who was a tough task master. It was clear that whoever got selected would be associated with him.

Gupta asked her one final question, "when can you join?" "Sir, within 30 days after recieving the offer letter". Most of the other officials asked her several personal questions but Gupta was a professional, he restrained from asking such questions. He was happy she proved to be fit for the job advertised by them.

Shivani was happy to get her offer letter which was almost double the salary she was earning. Moreover there was performance appraisal system in this company. She will stand to gain under this system as she was exceptionally a bright candidate. It was only because of her father's sudden demise she could not join MBA. She broke the news to her mother.

Gupta was very much satisfied with her work, though very professional he had a liking for Shivani. Whenever they worked late in the evenings, he made sure to drop Shivani at her home. Shivani used to invite him for a cup of tea, but he always refused, as he thought it is nice to keep employees at arm's length.

One day on her insistence he thought of breaking the rule; he accepted her invitation and went inside the home. He noticed the simple furniture, 3 to 4 chairs at a round table, a divan attached to the wall with nicely arranged cushions, there at the TV stand he could spot a photo probably Shivani's father's in a nice photo frame, close to that was a silver flower vase with fresh flowers in it.

Pointing towards the photo Shivani said, "Sir that's my dad's photo, I miss him very much. He always used to encourage me in whatever I do". Gupta was half listening to her. His attention was drawn to the lady who was standing in front of him. Shivani hugged her mother, and introduced her to her boss. "Sir this is my mother. She has suffered all her life to make two ends meet". Gupta was shocked to see in front of him his lost love. He could not believe his eyes. His head started spinning. He sat on the chair next to him. Shivani brought some water. Her mother too was very uneasy. Somehow he gathered himself; his professional approach to life helped him from falling prey to his emotions. He apologised and left.

Gupta could not believe what he saw. He never thought he would meet Nirmala again. Although he wished for it. He did not go to office for three days. Seeing Nirmala brought pleasant memories of the past. The silver flower vase was still there as a witness of their unflinching love for each other. It was presented to Nirmala on her birthday around twenty five years back.

Shivani noticed the change in Gupta, but it never crossed her mind, having some connection with her family and life.

Shivani asked for a week's leave, to go on a tour with her friends. Gupta granted her leave and offered financial help if she required. "Sir I will be back next Sunday, and hope you will have dinner at our place when I return". "Sure Shivani, wish you a happy journey".

All Gupta could think was of visiting Nirmala. He was dying to know how she lived since they last met each other.

Gupta mustered his courage and decided to at least meet Nirmala once. he in fact longed to meet her. He reached Shivani's house and pressed the calling bell.Nirmala opened the door, she was looking very normal, where as Gupta was restless. he did not know from where to start.

It was Nirmala who made him comfortable by offering a chair to sit. She brought some biscuits with tea. They talked on general matters and family issues. It was difficult for Nirmala in the early stages to adjust with life; she said she had a very loving husband, who struggled throughout his life to make them happy. He was a great husband and a loving father. She told him she has revealed everything to Shivani, about our past, if I hid things from her then I will be doing a dis service to her, 'because I revealed our past she has respect for our relation, if I had hidden and later on if she comes to know;it would upset her and create a permanent rift between mother and daughter. I have to get her married to a decent family before I close my eyes.I can't think anything beyond that.'

'I am proud of you Nirmala,even twenty five years back you were stronger than me , I feel proud of you, you are still the same strong Nirmala. I came here with a different reason, I wanted to see you, share the lost twenty five years time, ask you for some favours , man is always selfish, he does not understand the power and will of a woman, they are not ready to give them equal status but today I am sure it is not the question of giving equal status, women should be given more respect as they are more capable than men.'

'Let us be friends Nirmala, I am sure you have a generous heart to grant me with this request '

Someone entered the drawing room suddenly, it was Shivani...'sir can I call you dad'...It was a direct question; she had planned this after giving a lot of thinking. Just then Nirmala's and Gupta's eyes met, life was on a song.

"Life and times are difficult to understand, it is full of twists and turns.When some one gives us their time or spends time with us,they are giving part of their life to us,let us respect time."

7. Never underestimate.

Karim was a terror, all the shopowners,footpath dwellers,auto rickshaw owners all will have to give fixed amount regularly every month, his men knows how to collect those (haptha) money, no one dared to challenge him, it is said that even the local police was also on his mercy. Apart from this, though liquor is prohibited in this area it is freely available, it is supplied by him, and the local police also get its share.

He will walk in at any shop and get away with whatever things he wants. People were helpless as he had nexus with politicians as well. He was a very influential person, even certain complicated cases he has helped the police to solve.

Most of the time he will be sitting at a table outside 'Biss Millah restaurant' serving non vegetarian food. He regularly used to order mutton kheema and Bheja fry with roti.

He was at times very generous in gifting people, He was popular with the begging class, he will lavish food and cash on them, but when he gets irritant he will abuse them.

He had very smooth sailing now, but people say he had his struggling days too. When he was orphaned at a very young age, he did not get a proper job for survival, he had tough time even to get one square meal. Whatever he achieved now is on personal strength and courage. He has made a mark at which he does not pose a threat to his life style.

Very close to Bis Millah restaurant there was a small tea stall.As such in India at every ten step we find a tea stall catering the needs of all the shops,hospitals,offices, colleges, schools of that locality, people are addicted to tea, which is a gift given to us by British people when they ruled India for a very long period, It is unbelievable that hardly 18 to 20 thousand British soldiers controlled the 35 crore people of this land. Now we have grown to 125 crore in population

Every state government has abolished child labour, unfortunately we do not have any statistics ,as how many are engaged with these tea stalls,at all tea stalls child labour is engaged at alarming levels, It is time we make rules which we can implement.

So a boy of around 12 years old was working at the tea stall close to the 'Bis millah restaurant'. Karim used to tease this boy every now and then asking about his sister, others sitting along with him will laugh loudly enjoying these comments. The boy used to silently pass away without uttering anything this again encouraged them .One day again he made the mistake of asking the boy about his sister and teased him that ' tell her I will load her with gifts if she is ready to come with me.'

Karim had crossed the elastic limit, he chose a wrong day, the boy in a split second stabbed karim in the stomach several times and waved the knife towards his friends, who were caught off guard and did not know what to do.

The boy ran away with the knife from the site, Karim succumbed to his injuries on reaching the hospital.

One Karim died but another was born."Never under estimate , time is more powerful."

8. Bending the rules.

James is a retired Colonel from Indian Army, he had the good fortune to serve both Indian and British army,he had fought the Second World War in 1944-45.After retirement he was given land at western Gujarat. The land was very hard and sultry since it was close to the sea. It was a barren land, one can hardly find people at farming.

Most of the villagers had sold their land to the upcoming Industries, declaring their land for non agricultural use. There are agents who help you get your lands declared under this category.

James felt the villagers are lousy people, they are not interested in cultivation of their land but only interested in selling their land .They do not know how to invest their money for a regular return, they just booze and spend time in buying all those luxuries of life for which they were deprived, a good house, a motor bike or an Ambassador car.

Very soon people will come on the road either to work as farm labourer, as casual labourer at adjacent industries or engage themselves finding ways to generate easy money.

Many such farmers who lost their land were now working with Col.James. What a pity the owners have become servants.

Col.James's farm house was a modern and model farm house. He had nicely laid G.I. Pipes underground with opening at required places to water the plants, which can be managed by opening the valves fitted at key places. He had a Gobar gas plant which caters the power required. He was taking seasonal crops as well as regular plantation of fruits and vegetables. He had nearly three thousand birds, fifty milking buffalows.He had arranged musical system so that the buffalos yield more milk.

Col.James was leaving with his wife at the farm house. His evenings were pleasant, that is exclusively only for himself. He will open out the bottles and was very lavish in offering parties to his friends from the nearby naval base and Industries. He had developed good relations with the local government authorities, he was a quick learner to adjust to the civilian life style.

Many times he used to bring in the discussions with his friends about the bending of rules by Industrial giants, government authorities, and local people; sometimes he used to get disgusted with the corrupt system.

One day while coming back from the airport after leaving his wife, who left for Bangalore, it was getting dark, he did not notice a man who was walking at the side of the road was knocked down by his car. Col.James with the help of the few people gathered there took him to the hospital, the same day the man died. Police registered a case against Col.James.

The local villagers were angry with this incident, certain elements made several demonstrations, for the arrest of Col.James.Finally the police approached Col.James, his lawyer friends, police, and other friends all suggested finding a person who will be ready to take the entire blame on him.

His Industry friends found a poor old driver who was jobless due to old age and ill health,he was offered handsome money in exchange of submitting himself responsible for the accident which took place.

The deal was done, his starving family got a handsome amount, he was produced in the court for a hit and run case by police. The Judge listened to the lawyers, the evidence was placed before the court, and some villagers identified the person and confirmed the same in the court. The man was found guilty of rash driving taking the life of an old villager.

The driver's wife rushed to the court and shouted loudly at the judge , 'my husband is innocent, he is jobless for the past several months, he was at home all these days, please spare him, she produced the bundle of notes given to her husband, take this all but spare my husband!'

She was draged out from the court by the security staff; someone said she is mad, the entire village knows it.

The rules were twisted, unfortunately not by criminals but by learned people . I am sure Col.James must have consumed more pegs not in celebration but to forget this bad episode, which will never allow him that peace of mind.

9. Talent.

Dr.Philip Cameroon after taking his FRCS from London decided to devote his time at a faraway place where medical facility is scarce and poor.

He decided to work in India, which was at the time under British rule.

He choose to work in the state of Bihar .The people were poor, there was one general hospital, but the condition was very bad since no doctor's stayed for a long time, sufficient medicine supply was also not available.

Dr.Philip Cameroon streamlined everything, improved the quality of treatment, recruited adequate staff, and asked help from his government for funds, he took initiative in every field to improve the condition of hospitals not only for his district but also for other districts of Bihar. Soon Bihar was a model for medical facilities for other states.

The British government honoured Dr.Philip Cameroon by designating him as the chief of medical and health services for the state of Bihar. His work among the poor and needy was louded by 'World health organisation.'

Today he was tired after a very complicated tumour operation of an old lady. It took almost two hours to get through, he was constantly monitoring the health condition of the patient. He was satisfied with the progress made by the patient.

Now he was in a relaxed mood, he called the theatre boy Ramdas to his cabin.

Ramdas has been working in this hospital for the past 10 years, ever since Dr.Philip joined the hospital. At that time it was a village dispensary, which had grown in to a district level well equipped hospital. He joined Dr.Philips at the age of sixteen years; soon after passing his 10th standard. Ramdas joined the hospital, assisted every one, mainly Dr.Philip. He never got a promotion or monetary benefit other than the regular salary. He never looked at the watch, always worked till Dr.Philip remained in the hospital.

Dr.Philip would instruct him and give a list of tools to be made available for the operation on the previous day, accordingly Ramdas used to sterilize the tools and place it in the operation theatre.

Dr.Philip Cameroon looked at Ramdas lowering his specs , "Tell me Ramdas, I did not ask you for certain additional tools for the operation today, what prompted you to keep those additional tools in the theatre".

In the operation theatre when the operation was in progress , Dr.Philip was looking very tense at a certain point, just then Ramdas handed over the special tool to doctor who took it from him and completed the operation, it was this that he was referring to Ramdas.

"Sir, eight years back we carried a similar type of operation, at that time you ordered to keep ready the special tools in case of any complications, I did not ask you but I thought I will keep the tools ready in case we require them".

Dr.Philip got up from his chair, shook hands with Ramdas, and told him, "You are a doctor", Ramdas was surprised what happened next was history.

Dr.Philip took up his case with his government in London,Ramdas was sent to UK for further studies, he was given special coaching in English, joined the university, cleared his graduation in medicine , and finally became an FRCS. He came back to India after several years.

The entire hospital staff welcomed him for his achievement. He joined the same hospital with humbleness. Dr.Philip Cameroon in his retirement speech emphasised the need for dedication and devotion in this profession. He lauded the achievement of Dr.Ramdas, from a theatre boy to the position of a chief medical and health services post by his sheer hard work and devotion.

“One must use talent with great humility otherwise it will develop a desire for power and activate arrogance in our attitude.”

10. Lady of the evening.

Bajaj was a very industrious and successful marketing personnel. Give him any product he can create a market for it. He was the most wanted marketing executive.

Nothing succeeds like success, but success boosts your ego, you become arrogant. This arrogance reflects in your personal as well as professional life.

It is normal and common with the marketing people or sales people that, they make friends very easily, for which they always give credit to their bad habits such as boozing and smoking more than their marketing skills.

This temporary habit becomes a regular habit; you reach a point from where you cannot return.

Bajaj from an ordinary sales clerk scaled new heights in marketing. Along with his job he acquired the required qualifications to achieve success.

He was constantly travelling to different places, interacting with different people, achieving all the difficult targets. He was number one in the marketing world.

Bajaj was very flamboyant by nature, he was attached to three vices, the three 'W's': wealth, wine and women. A habit he cultivated in his professional life. This disturbed his personal life to some extent. He was unable to share any time with his family. His arrogant nature distanced him from his wife and daughter. Even when in town he will be reaching home very late, that too in a drunken state.

Bajaj had cut short relations with his own brothers and sisters because of his arrogant nature. At times his brother's approached him for financial help, but he will flatly refuse, according to him every individual should manage their finances accordingly, so that they need not ask for a loan from someone.

One day while on a business trip to Mumbai, he stayed at the same five star hotel where he regularly used to stay. Most of the room service boys knew him and his habits. He used to tip them heavily, as the company used to reimburse the entire expences. He was even eligible for out of pocket expenses.

The usual pimp approached him in the hotel room and offered to bring a new girl for his pleasure tonight. He left the room after having a peg of whisky offered by Bajaj. Bajaj had already washed down five pegs and was waiting for the arrival of a new bird, by the pimp.

He opened the door and asked the pimp and the girl to come in. The girl covered her face with a scarf, the pimp collected his fees and left the scene.

Bajaj in a semi conscious state, pulled the girl towards him forcefully, the girl was reluctant , she with equal force pushed Bajaj to the floor. He was very furious, Nobody dared to behave like this. The girl desperately tried to open the door and run away. Bajaj got violent and attempted to stop the girl. Just then the girl uncovered the scarf from her face.

Bajaj was dumb struck as the girl was his own daughter. He was in a state of shock. His daughter opened the door and gave herself up from the nineth floor balcony.

Bajaj had a massive heart attack and collapsed, his daughter took her life instantly. Sometimes we pay a very high price for crossing the moral code.

'One life should be enough to learn, never compromise on values and ethics.'

11. Divorce.

Ved Prakash is in his eighties. Struggle is not the word to be used, he is a fighter through out his life, and will never give up hope.

Malati, his wife always supported him and stood as a rock behind him. They lost their only son in a road accident.

He lost his job in the thirties, according to him he was wrongfully removed from service, a case he is still fighting. There was a compromise deal to withdraw the case against a fairly decent compensation, but he refused. Ved Prakash was a man of principle. He would never give up until he makes his point clear.

He had no savings. He did odd jobs to survive, in the hope that one day he will win the case and his honour will be restored, he can walk with his head held high.

The judicial system is very slow, too many cases with limited courts and judges.

His friends used to advice him, "look, enough of this struggle. When they are ready to offer a fairly decent compensation, why are you so adamant?". He had to change his lawyer three times as they too felt its not going to yield any good result for him; the employer is a very powerful and influential person. At any cost he is not going to take him back on the company rolls.

Ved Prakash was a tough nut to crack. He wanted to win this case. He told his friends, "I only wish to work at least a day in the office, after which I am ready to resign'.

The union which was backing him also withdrew their support. He faught his case alone. Slowly people around him,his friends and relatives branded him arrogant and egoistic. They distanced themselves from him. The only encouragement and support he got was from his wife Malati.

Malati is five years younger to him; she is seventy five years old. She is sick and looks very tired. Ved Prakash is very old and he can merely walk with the help of a walking stick. He still goes to the grocery shop to copy down the daily sales and expenditure in the accounts book. The shop owner was nice to him as Ved Prakash completes the daily entries before leaving for home.

Life is miserable for some. At the age of eighty, when his faculties are giving up one by one, his failing vision, his hearing is partially blocked, he lost most of his teeth, he is still working. Even Malati has no rest, she doesn't have a helping hand. Sometimes when alone Malati would cry in silence remembering her son. If he was still alive, he would have been of great help to them. He would have been married and taken care of the house. Life is full of if's and but's.The truth is they are stretching life beyond the tolerable limit.

Both Malati and Ved Prakash spent time talking about their fate. They are now just pulling their life. There is nothing they can do except wait for their time to get over.

Malati's health was deteriorating very fast. She had many complications, but she is a strong willed lady, that's how she pulled this far. Many of her sufferings she concealed from her husband as she never wanted to load him with more worries. One day before leaving for the shop Ved Prakash noticed, Malati was struggling for breath, he immediately took her to the hospital. She went through series of medical tests.

The doctor's attending on her informed that she has to go for a bypass surgery at the earliest, as she has three blockages.

Ved Prakash had taken her to a private hospital, as he knew the conditions of the government hospitals are very poor. Government after government has failed to improve the quality of treatment. Most of the hospitals are ill equipped, unhygienic and only the helpless poor would visit these hospitals.

The Hospital authorities asked Ved Prakash to deposit two lakh rupees for the operation and hospitalisation expences. Ved Prakash had no money. He contacted a known trustee for the facility of paying the charges in instalments. They said they cannot waive the rules for an individual; "you will have to deposit the money before they start the treatment. If you wish I can ask the authorities to give you two days time to arrange the money.'

Among all the difficulties and challenges of life this was the toughest. He silently prayed to God to show him a way out of this. "God I have never asked you for any favour in my life, not even beg for mercy for the employment I lost. I never questioned when you took away my son in an accident, I was strong enough to withstand all the sufferings, sorrows imposed on me. Today I am at your door step for this unfortunate desciple, who always trusted you, regular in her rituals and prayers, it is a test of your existence. I am aware nobody can avert death, but I wish to try everything possible to save her, because I will be failing in my duty as her husband if I do not try everything possible at my disposal. I cannot be a silent spectator to her sufferings. I cannot see her dying with out getting the treatment. She has lived with me through thick and thin. I must succeed in getting her a decent treatment, otherwise it will be your failure, it will be your defeat God."

He approached the trustee again, who explained that there is a clause in the rules of the hospital, if she is an orphan or a divorcee with nobody to support, she will get free medical treatment.

This small piece of information energised the old veins of Ved Prakash with hope. He contacted an influential lawyer for a divorce suit with mutual understanding and consent to proceed to obtain clearance from the court so that Malati can get the treatment.

Ved Prakash took the paper to Malati, "listen my dear, we are in to our golden jubilee marriage anniversary, and all these years you were a silent sufferer of my doings. I have not given you any happiness in life. My arrogance and self pride perhaps destroyed your aspirations. I failed to understand or acknowledge your dreams of life. I never tried to understand that you too had a life of your own. On the contrary you always supported me. I wish to restore everything for you. I wish to do everything possible to free you from this physical suffering and there is only one way to do it. Unless we take a mutual divorce, it is not possible. Its only for the authorities who wish to have them on a piece of paper as a proof of our separation. I want to get it only for the sake of saving your life. I wish to live the rest of my life only for you. Please sign these papers, the time is running out, this is only a formality. We are one, no power on earth can separate us."

Malati, told him, "I have always obeyed you and acted as per your wish. Why do you say that you have not given any happiness? I am proud to be your wife, you were my strength. I used to enjoy the struggle shouldering the burden with you. Tell me where to sign."

They got the divorce. It was a great relief for Ved Prakash, that this divorce has saved Malati's life. The God has shown a way to save her life.

After fifty years of legal battle finally Ved Prakash won the case. The court ordered to pay him the entire arrears payment till his retirement age. Ved Prakash was garlanded by his friends and unions on his victory.

Ved Prakash met the hospital trustees and paid the medical bill of Malati. He formed a trust with the union leaders to help the poor for medical aids.

"If my savings can bring happiness in the life of my suffering brothers and sisters, there is no greater prayer than parting away from my belongings, hence I donate my entire money to this trust, I am not the owner of this property or money , I am only a trustee."

A portion of his house was converted in to the office of the trust.

'The joy of giving is so different, give until it hurts.'

12. Dream.

It was scary, under the rough sea, coming up on the waves for a few seconds for fresh breath, moving at lightning speed.

It is beyond my imagination, It was large and spacious, with small compartments, fishes, plants, glittering stones along with a variety of colourful beings. It was moving swiftly, was it a submarine or a ship? No it wasn't, It was as if I was travelling inside the womb of a big fish.

There were occasional glimpses of trees and houses; certain familiar scenes, but again those mighty waves, waves that brought with it thousands of tiny fishes, all that got inside, some of it remained within, trapped as it is struggling to get out, waiting for the next opening of the giant mouth, gasping for fresh breath. The hollowness inside was slippery. I could not understand as to how and why I was there. I felt the fright, I didn't know what to do, my voice was choked, I was unable to shout. It terrorized me, my heart was pounding at rapid speed, I was scared of the mighty waves, the sea was in a mood to gulp me. How many times it touched the bottom, again surged up determined. Was it a mighty whale or a ferocious shark? I do not know. All I knew was that I wasn't comfortable inside it, every bit within me was dying with fear.

The inside was like a prison. There was a grilled window; may be the fins of this giant creature through which I was peeping out, I was panick stricken, with palpitating heartbeats ,unsteady breaths, sleepless eyes, trying to figure out what it means. Why am I suffering? Why am I travelling inside this giant fish? How do I come out of it/ I was really scared.

Looking through the window, the blue waters, splashing all around, no escape at sight, I cried loudly. This time somehow my voice found its way only to wake my mom. I was sweating in the bed. My mom took me in her arms and told me in my ear, "Don't worry dear I am here". I was silent, reassured, I am in the safe hands, protected from all evil thoughts, the disturbing dream, the bad dream.

It came repeatedly, regularly for many days and months, every time I was safely protected in my mother's arms. Finally one day the dreams stopped coming me. It no more scarred me. I was capable of dealing with it. I am grown up now, no dream can scare me.

The reality of life disturbed me. This is my new dilemma. I am again in the same mould, terrorized, scarred, and disturbed. It is not a dream; it is the life's reality.

The fight against terror, poverty, injustice, evil forces, corrupt administration, shattering of dreams of our freedom fighters, responsibility to restore the order in society, struggle of mankind for survival, deprived of one meal a day, the hunger, the discremation of cast system, the growing unemployment, no shelter, living at a make shift shed at the sides of a footpath, under a bridge or inside abandoned huge old pipe pieces!

Where are we heading to wards development? The rich is growing richer, the poor is pushed back down the poverty line. They say rupees thirty two for urban poor is enough or rupees twenty six for poor villagers per day for survival. Look at the numbers, more than 40 crores in India alone below this poverty line, how can they survive?

Can they provide nutritional food to their children? What legacy is left for our future generation/ All just a dream, a dream unfulfilled for my countrymen. It is a long wait. The hopes are dying, aspirations dying, happiness taking a back seat, sufferings, sickness, poverty at the forefront.

Why do people lose their temper? Why do they become naxalites? Why are their lands forcefully taken away? When will they get the real freedom? When the dream gets converted to reality, this itself is a big dream of hope!!

The reality scares me more than the childhood dreams, the poor the down trodden live in the prison of time. There should be some mechanism to protect the poor, their children from hunger, malnutrition.

We must provide a decent environment for our next generation for their growth, otherwise we will be making their life miserable.

13. Survival.

Ranjan Desai retired from service ten years back. He was working with a private company. After his graduation he joined the firm as a clerk. After putting in 35 years of service he retired without getting a promotion, except for some salary hikes by way of annual increment.

It is not that he was not competent enough for a promotion but he was the victim of likes and dislikes by his seniors. His seniors changed frequently, as they were all highly qualified professionals looking for a change every two years for better prospects.

All the seniors who work with Ranjan will initially have problems, but when they leave the company they will have high praise for Ranjan. No doubt Ranjan Desai was a very intelligent, sincere, hard working person, but he was not in the good books of the management because of his open nature. He will never hesitate to call a spade a spade.

The management had no complaint of his work, but his attitude was a problem. He never had an adjusting nature. He will insult any senior if they go wrong; this attitude displeased most of his colleagues.

Rajan Desai had no children; his wife was suffering from many health issues. This may be the reason why he was irritant most of the time.

It is not only the work ability that counts, our attitude also matters. When we compare two employees for promotion there are several factors taken in to consideration. Ranjan lost to his competitor every time there was a vacancy for promotion. The promotion committee always thought that they will be facing more problems if they promote Ranjan for higher responsibility. Ranjan reached to a point where he was now not even refered for promotion.

This lead to frustration. He was terribly dissatisfied with life. He had no house of his own. A good portion of his savings were spent on the treatment of his wife.

The employer was a very influential person. He could get any work done in the government offices. He was not afraid of any rules or legislations. He was smart enough to find his way through the toughest regulations. He was at his best to bribe the government agencies and officers. Even some of his Industrial friends also used his skill for their advantage.

This has deprived most of the employees from the benefit passed by the government for the betterment of the working class. We have many legislation for the benefit of working class but the benefits are not passed to them. The implementation part by the government is very poor.

Ranjan Desai did not get much benefit from the employer, as a result after retirement he was again working part time with private agencies for a living.

Ranjan was tired of the present life, he was just pulling for the sake of passing time, and his wife was suffering from heavy depression because of her heavy medication. At times both husband and wife will sit back to compare their life with other people, who are placed in much better way.

Comparing oneself with others is always futile. It is your approach to life that matters. One must know how to be happy in life. Most of the time it is our attitude which distances us from others. We must love people to attract them towards us. The moment we drift away from people, we distance ourself from the loved ones and will always remain in self imprisonment.

Ranjan Desai's wife suffered a heart attack but survived. She was under complete bed rest, Ranjan looked after his wife in all possible manners, he was giving her the regular exercise as per the instruction of the physiotherapist. Now she was on road to complete recovery.

Ranjan had no desire to live, he had this melancholic feeling of ending his life, many times he thought of committing suicide, but the thought of his sick wife never permitted him to do so. He was just pulling life,he has to complete the time and life granted to him, how long is the big question bothering him.

Ranjan Desai's wife can now move about in the house, she started to attend the kitchen duties also, they always cooked for both the times at one go, her neighbours used to help her, feeling pity for this old couple. Doctor had warned her not to strain much, one more shock will take her life; so she must be always kept at ease.

Mrs.Ranjan Desai was looking through her window, it was evening time, the sky was clear, the sun was moving towards the west by changing its colour, it was getting radiant and gave up its power,hiding behind the clouds.Some people were approaching towards her house, there were known faces as well as unknown faces, all gathered and assembled at the entrance of the house.

An elderly person approached Mrs.Desai and broke the news, 'Ranjan is no more, he fainted in the market area,was taken to a doctor who pronounced and declared him as dead.' Some older ladies gathered around Mrs.Desai, who was in a state of shock, she was not crying, she slowly walked towards her cot and silently lied down.The ladies gathered around her to console her,since she was not crying they needed to give her some sort of a shock so as to make her cry and vent out her sorrow.She was stone like lying in front of them, she was not listening to them. Some of the ladies were very emotional and crying by feeling pity for this old couple, some ladies were crying artificialy as it is a custome to exhibit their sorrow in such circumstances.

The neighbours brought the body of Ranjan and placed it in the front room, there was a sudden loud cry, she was weeping, she thought the world is very cruel,God has no mercy the only support she had is taken away,she has no place to go,she was profusely crying, unconsolable.

Ranjan's body was prepared for the final rites to be performed at the river front,all the preparations were done, and his distant relative too arrived to light the funeral pyre

Suddenly someone noticed a movement,some one shouted there is life,Rajan is alive, people rushed to the spot, untied the knots, made him sit, gave him water.

Ranjan was surprised, he was looking all around.Someone ran home and whispered the news to one of the lady at Ranjan's house. The entire atmosphere changed dramatically, unbelievable!! The dead man has come alive a miracle ?

Rajan Desai has come back to life, next day's paper he was in the headlines; the poor doctor was at the receiving end, he was the talk of the town.

Ranjan Desai was alive and so his wife, she withstood the greatest shock in spite of one heart attack earlier, Is it to be believed that she is cured of her heart problem?

Both of them whispered to each other,now what is in store for us,some more daily survival issues,once again we will have to go through the grind, how long...

The state went under the governor's rule; he was a seasoned upright man knowing all the nexus between the political leaders and the Business community. He knew the prevailing corrupt system;he ordered the enforcement team to strictly comply all the irregularities. Several Business houses were raided, several arrests were made, the working class finally got their justice from the Governor's rule, very unfortunate they did not benefit from their legislative representatives.

Ranjan Desai too got some of the pending dues,finally the survival has come with a package, never say never again.

Life is unpredictable; no one can say what is in store for them.'Truth shall always prevail'.

14. Re-union.

"Why are we against Pakistan papa?" This was the question Nayna the 20 year old college going daughter asked her father. Niranjan looked at his daughter, raising his head from the morning news paper, "my dear you will get late for your college; it is a long history of hatred and partisan between these two countries. You must have studied in school and college, known from your teachers everything about this, you are not a kid now."

"But Papa, what I understand from everyone is that the Muslims are not reliable; they will always side with Pakistan even when a cricket match is played between our two countries, they have a liking and an inclination towards Pakistan though they live in India."

"Now you go to college we will discuss this in the evening, there is truth in what some people say. But let me tell you, not the entire community is to be blamed for this. There are exceptions. The youth of this community is mislead by certain elements in the society that triggers hatred."

Nayna took her scooter and started for college. At the signal she noticed that the rear tyre of her scooter was flat. She dragged her scooter to a nearby puncture shop near the petrol pump, as she knew the owner Antony.

"Uncle please get it quickly fixed, I am getting late for my college", "Ten minutes Nayna, let me finish this, he is a doctor, he too is getting late; lot of patients are waiting for him."

"No problem uncle I can wait". The unfinished thoughts of the morning came back to her mind. She asked instantly without any reference, "Now tell me uncle, why India and Pakistan cannot come together? Why do we blame Muslims for all the terrorist attacks? Why do we look down upon them?"

"Listen Nayna, at one breath you asked many vital questions, you will have to get back to the partisan time to understand the bitterness between these two communities".

"You know Dr.Haroon who left just now, is very popular among his patients. For him all his patients are equal. The hatred comes out of bitterness, we should spread the message of love in the society".

Nayna's scooter was ready. She got an important lead from an 8th standard school drop out, a simple man toiling 12 hours a day. She found Antony uncle more learned compared to the more learned people she has interacted including her teachers.

She met her friends in the cafeteria, carrying the same topic. Everyone had different opinions, but one thing was common: they all held the Muslims of India responsible to some extent, as according to them they could have opted Pakistan instead of living in India.

While the students were having this discussion Professor Bajpai entered the canteen. Though in his fifties he always mingled with the students freely and guide them with valuable tips to succeed in life. He was a very practical person, never afraid of spelling out what he thought to be correct.

Professor was dragged in to this discussion on the hindu vs muslim topic. Proffessor was very cool to react, "I am by birth a hindu, a Muslim too is by birth a muslim, did any of us know this, the day we were born? These religions are man made, we should not give much importance to it. We must live in harmony above caste and religious lines".

Nayna interrupted, "But sir why do we look down upon the Muslims living in India!"

You are right Nayna ,"You look at the Industrial belt in your state. There are thousands of large, medium and small scale Industries, barring few big Industrial houses like Tata's and Birla's. Most of them avoid employment opportunities to muslims. When you interview a person for any particular job, you always think on the religious line. Look at the Muslims, you will find them doing all types of jobs: selling fruits and vegetables, as rickshaw drivers, at hotels, tea stalls, bakeries, as casual labourers, etc. They are struggling but will establish themselves in the future. Their circumstances has taught them the hard lessons of life. And even in them there are exceptions, some get derailed".

Nayna was very delighted to talk to Professor Bajpai, who gave a new direction to the youngsters. He asked them to come out of prejudice to challenge the authorities from discrimination on religious lines.

They all parted to attend their classes. The college was over and Nayna along with her friend Karishma headed for their home. They got a phone call that their class mate Rajesh is admitted in a private nursing home due to viral fever. They thought of paying a visit to Rajesh, they headed for the nursing home.

When they entered the room, Nayna saw Dr.Haroon. Both of them immediately exchanged greetings as they just met each other at Antony's puncture shop. Rajesh was suffering for the past 3 to 4 days but he took it lightly hence feeling very weak. Dr.Haroon consoled his mother, "Aunty don't worry. He will be alright within a couple of days". Just when he was leaving, Nayna asked him if she can meet him for a few minutes to clear some points. The doctor agreed but only after half an hour during the lunch break.

Nayna wanted to clear certain doubts bothering her mind, but probably she never knew the political clout and seriousness which existed between these two nations.

She approached Dr.Haroon for his comments on the issue. Dr.Haroon smiled at her incrusitiveness. He began explaining: "Madam, I am very much impressed with your question in all its sincerity. You are aware of the British policy of divide and rule. They gave us freedom to a united India. By dividing this great country in to two parts creating chaos, the birth of India and Pakistan, there were violence we cannot imagine, brutal massacres, killing each other, finally we were separated, that generation suffered to full fill the unrealistic ambition of certain politicians and individuals. History will never pardon them, this even took the life of Mahatma Gandhi.

Now two generations down, across the two countries the general public has no bitterness, but surely between the governments it still persists. As such from the sports field, cultural, literature field, film freternities,TV artists and the common people from both countries wish to come closer for better understanding. Cultural exchange is the best solution; this generation has already moved ahead of partisan era, it is up to us to take it forward. The people across the border are our own brothers and sisters; it is time we realize that".

Nayna was impressed, and happy. In a day she gathered lot of information on this subject from the common people of her country.

She reached home in a very happy mood. It was dinner time, all of them gathered around the table. Nayna's brother too reached from office. Nayna's mother took up the topic, to finalise the date of Nayna's marriage as they had received a phone from overseas with a marriage proposal. As the boy is coming on a short leave from US, they will have to make a quick engagement followed by marriage.

They finalized the dates according to their convenience and Niranjan conveyed the same to Nayna's would be In-laws.

Nayna was sometimes very demanding. After the telephone call she asked her father, "Papa when will we invite uncle and family for the marriage?"

Niranjan looked at Nayna in surprise. He was angry. There is nothing left between him and his brother after the demise of their parents on a property dispute 15 years ago. Nayna was just a child at the time. Maya, Nayna's mother too suggested it is not a bad idea. Niranjan was furious, "you do not understand, he will never come on the contrary, he will insult us".

Nayna was adamant "Papa we talk about many things about partition of India and Pakistan. Here it is between you two brothers. We must reunite spitting all the vermin from our system. After all, he is your younger brother".

Maya also supported, "These are the occasions when the family gets united. We will be inviting several people from Vishnu's locality. Not inviting them will only further deepen the hatred. Let us make this occasion to patch up the differences.'

Nayna's brother sided with his father, he said "I have no objection if they are invited, but it should be left to Papa, he is the person who suffered the most. I do not know who was at more fault, but I will always stand by my Papa".

The marriage date approached, Niranjan was adamant. Probably his ego never allowed him for a truce with his brother. Ego destroys our relations from coming close to each other. He strictly warned his family members not to go against his wish.

Nayna was a rebel, she secretly visited her uncle Vishnu's house, they welcomed her cordially. As a child she played in the tender care of her uncle, how can she forget this? She narrated the stories Vishnu used to tell her. She informed them about her marriage date. All of them including her cousins were surprised to see her. They were happy about her marriage, and it was a thrill to revisit the lost relatives.

Niranjan's were for a surpise. Two days before the marriage, Vishnu's entire family came to stay with them. As if Niranjan too wanted it to happen this way, he welcomed all of them. It was a happy reunion.The new generation thinks in a different way, Nayna was very much happy her marriage was instrumental in bringing two families together.

Deep inside her something was ringing, Dr.Haroon's words "The people across the border are our own brothers and sisters. it is time we realize that". There is hope for a bright tomorrow.

15. New lease of life.

"Why should I live now? My death will not make a difference to any one. No one is bothered whether I live or die". He decided to commit suicide.

He thought life is very unkind to him, all relations are breaking up, he has no place to go, why should he drag this life, waiting for death? Why not to end it?

These were the thoughts going on in the mind of fifty year old Jaswanth. Life is a great disappointment for him. He joined army but could not complete the required number service to qualify for pension, he had to quit his service due to many personal reasons.

After coming back to his village in Gujarat he started farming. They were four brothers. They could not cultivate the land jointly as they got separated due to family dispute and in fighting. Three of his brothers sold their land to a giant Industrial house for a handsome compensation. Jaswanth was reluctant to sell his land as he thought the easy money will be lost very fast. A land is a traditional investment, it is an address for his children, an identity in the society. He wanted to do farming but failure of monsoon for three consecutive years put him in a fix.

He was unable to repay the loans taken from the bank, the interest was mounting high. He tried to borrow money from his brothers who refused to lend him under one pretext or the other.

All his brothers shifted to city area and purchased bungalows and luxury cars with all modern amenities.The villagers were much impressed by their lifestyle. They too were looking for prospective buyers.The land sharks, the middlemen were all busy negotiating with prospective buyers. The major chunk of money was going in to the pocket of these middlemen.

There were ample examples of villagers who lost their money in a couple of years, by spending all their wealth after luxury cars and by starting wrong business about which they were less experienced and ill informed. They live on the streets now in search of jobs and some of them are employed at the same premises as labourers of which they were owners once.

Jaswanth tried all efforts to come out of the situation. He was not willing to sell the land. He had difference of opinion with his family members over the land. They too were of the opinion to dispose the land. Jaswanth was thinking on a different line. His family failed to understand him. When he goes to his brothers for a loan, they try advising him, "Jassu you are unnecessarily putting yourself in trouble. Why don't you dispose the land? How long will you beg for money from others? You try to manage your affairs yourself".

Jaswanth decided to end his life.He thought 'Let everyone be happy by selling the land after my demise, why should I be a hurdle. When your own people are not ready to listen to you, what is the meaning of your life!!'

It was evening time and getting dark, the sun already disappeared from the horizon letting the darkness to take charge, Jashwanth reached the bridge to bring end to all his worries, problems and his precious life. He decided to jump in the river by tying a large stone around his neck giving double effect to make sure he will not survive in his attempt to commit sucide. The noose with the rope will tighten his neck and the stone tied to the rope will surely take him down to the bottom of the river, only to resurface after death.

He was silently getting ready, escaping the attentions of the by passers; as such who has the time to look at all these, all are running for their jobs or to their homes.

Once again Jaswanth thought, am I selfish to think of ending my life? He remembered when bad time approaches even our shadow will desert us.

From the other end of the bridge someone climbed on the parapet and jumped with a huge cry. Jashwanth could not make out clearly, but was sure some one jumped from the bridge. Some people gathered to look from the bridge, no one dared to jump to save the person, Jaswanth immediately removed the rope around his neck and jumped in to the river. He dived many times to spot the person, he was frantically swimming, diving and finally caught hold of the person and swam back to the shore.

His military training came handy for him. He pumped out the water from the stomach of the lady. She was very young. She gained consciousness, she was very weak to say anything. She was puzzled. People gathered around and tried to comfort her.

The police arrived and asked Jaswanth to be present at the police station the next day for his statement.

Jaswanth was a relaxed man now. He knew how precious this life is. Why did he save her, when he himself was trying to take his life?

He was not in a position to advice the lady about anything like others, for the simple reason that he was destined to save her life. What led him to reach the spot ultimately saved two lives; but who knew!!

Jaswanth is no more a coward to run away from life. He proved himself a hero. He was the only one from the crowd to dive to the depth of the river to rescue a lady from the jaws of defeat and death, he is a hero today.

16. Moving forward.

Sunil was the CEO of a multinational company. After his degree in engineering, he did his MBA from IIM Ahmedabad.

It took him five years to reach to this position. He is from a very ordinary lower middle class family. His father Ravindra was working as an artisan in a private company. Ravindra made it sure, at any cost he will avail best of education to his son.

Sunil was an exceptionally bright student. He always used to come first in the class right from primary classes.

Sunil did his Engineering from a Regional Engineering college. There he met Sheila, who was also in the same class. She too completed her degree along with Sunil. Sheila was from a different back ground, her parents were in the civil service and very rich with affluent culture.

Sheila's parents agreed for the marriage as they found that Sunil is a very intelligent qualified person. Since both of them were in love with each other, they agreed to their marriage. From Sunil's side his parents had slight reservation as they wished Sunil should marry from their own community, that he should bring luck to a girl from their community.

Sunil did not face any stiff opposition from his parents, their marriage was solemnised with every one's blessings.

Sheila was employed in a government job as an executive engineer and worked for two years before getting married to Sunil.

Sheila was a very adjustable wife and daughter in-law. She started taking interest in changing the set up of the house from the lower middle class to the level of Sunil's position. She was bringing the changes very slowly as she knew she will face opposition if she suddenly try to change things. Whatever she did she got approved by her in-laws. Sunil's parents were very happy with Sheila for her this quality and understanding.

Sheila had taken charge of the house. She changed the interior of the house, the kitchen was completely redone and she served delicious new receipies to the family from the traditional lower middle class food habits. All these things she did without disturbing the family fabric and likings. Sunil was very happy as he had no botheration at the domestic front. She was handling everything very smoothly.

They were staying in a rented house. Sheila made sure they moved to their own house.They purchased a new car, new furniture for their home, they made several financial deposits for generating extra money for the future of their children's education. She gave birth to twins, a baby boy and a girl.

Sheila took care of Sunil's parents, taking them for regular health checkups. She even took them for moderate exercise and walking to the nearby park. Her children now started going to school. She devoted her entire time to the house and family.

All the neighbours and friends used to praise her efforts in bringing prosperity in the life of their small family. Sunil's father and mother had all the praise for Sheila. They never failed to consult her for any matter, she was a darling of the house.

Good times never last long, that is the rule if everyone is happy on this earth for a very long time nobody will spare a moment for God.

It was Sunil's birthday and Sheila forced Sunil to accompany her to buy some gift for all family members. They were going through the highway to a famous mall which had come up recently.

Suddenly in order to save a rough bike rider, Sunil turned the steering full circle only to collide with the side lamp post. Sheila was thrown out of the car her head hitting on the mile stone, she died on the spot. Sunil was safe because of the safety belt.

It was a tragic blow to the family. It was a great loss to her children. It was a shock to the entire society. She had won the hearts of every one with her pleasing personality and manners.

Days passed, as Sunil is still young, there were offers for marriage even from girls young and beautiful. Everything was past now, his parents were also keen to get him married. Sunil was also thinking about his young kids, finally the thought of re-marrying crossed his mind.

A new leaf in life, everything forgotten, no one is indispensable, keep moving that is the tradition, some may not get married again, some may think the other way, nobody can claim who is right and who is wrong.

The things will move but it will never be the same.

17. Retirement.

It is evening time, the sun sliding down towards west, the sea is calm, but roaring sound marks the emergence of high tide, the blue sky is painted reddish, birds chirping signalling the end activities for the day flying towards it's nest, at far away we can hear the wild cry of foxes on their hunting expedition,at some places we can spot the wild boar coming out of the thick green belt area to drink water from the water shed, the day's activities coming to an end but certainly there are activities reserved for the night too.

The activities never end from cradle to grave;one has to do something or the other,after retirement you plan about doing something which you missed while in active service.Ranganathan too is retiring from service today, he has many plans, he wish to persue his hobbies like writing poems and stories, visiting places, he wish to spend more time with his wife;she always used to complain about his absence in most of the family functions back at Chennai because of his work demand.

Employees of a giant Industrial group assembled at the venue at Sea shore to give a send off party to Ranganathan, who is retiring from service after thirty five years of service, it is a great achievement at a time when people are changing jobs frequently at regular intervels, and this is a rare happening.

It was a moment to honour Ranganathan for his dedicated service and more so the management wish to confer on him a long service award.

Ranganathan was working with the accounts department; he was also associated with other initiatives introduced by the management along with other social activities, like the co operative stores, clubs run by the company. He was usually entrusted with the responsibility of a treasurer, as he is a confident and capable accountant.

Ranganathan is a serious critic of cricket, even in the office he used to criticise colleagues who takes leave to watch a live cricket match. Most of the time the club authorities face difficult questions from Ranganathan as he disapproves the sports fund only spent on cricket.

Today every one assembled to give a fitting send off to their friend and colleague on the last working day of Ranganathan.

Ranganathan was welcomed by the co-ordinator of the event, followed by personal experience of his collegues, some narrated funny and humours experiences they had with Ranganathan.

Listening to his collegues, Ranganathan became very emotional, he rose to address the gathering in a choked voice, 'Friends, please forgive me if I have done anything wrong in my 35 years of long association, I have deliberately never done anything against any of you, if I have received promotion; believe me I have not snatched it away from any of my friends, I have never jumped the que.. My wife always used to complain that I am not devoting time for the family as I am always busy with work and after working hours busy with the other social activities, I have to give my time to my wife, she should not have any further complaints, I will spend maximum time with her, we will go for movies, outings and places which we have not yet visited.'

After his speech many others shared the Dias to praise the other qualities of Ranganathan. He is a good writer and always used to write articles on various touching issues of the society, they also wished him to pursue this hobby after retirement.

The party was over by eleven o'clock in the night, after which everyone departed for their homes.

Next day morning Ranganathan got up early as usual, only to be reminded by his wife that he is retired and he need not get up so early. He could not help years of cultivated habit, he cannot get rid of it instantly, he tried to lie down for a while, but he got up went for the morning news paper and waited for the usual morning tea which he got very late today.

His wife shouted from the kitchen, 'listen please take Malay to the block 1, his school bus will come any time from now', oh! Suddenly he realised he has to take his grandson Malay to the school bus, as both his son and daughter in law are office going people.

He came back, brushed , took bath and waited for his breakfast which came very late, Now he understood the busy hectic daily activities in the house during the morning hours, as he was always the first person to leave for office in the morning.

His daughter in law assigned him another work, 'Papa when Malay comes from school in the afternoon please check his home work diary and make him complete it.'.

The order came from the kitchen, 'now you come out of the room and sit in the varandah, let the maid clean the rooms. 'With out any protest as an obedient student he silently waited for the maid to finish her mopping. Normally he carried the news paper to the office and in-between the breaks he used to read them fully, now the paper is also in the room, he thought let her complete there after I can settle with the paper.

His wife reached the varandah and told that she could not get the vegetables and fruits yesterday so he will have to go for it, as such she is relieved as he can help her in reducing her burden. In the scroching heat he went to the market, came back with the list of fruits and vegetables, while keeping them in the fridge his wife casually asked him, 'how much is for apple for a kg?' Ranganathan had no answer to this question, he was fumbling, he had no experience of going to market, as all these work were managed by his wife all these years.

When she did not get an answer she just said loudly, 'what kind of an accountant you are, you buy something and you don't know the price? 'Half of the vegetables are a spoiled lot, means you paid double the price for less quantity

It was almost 10.30 in the morning , normally he gets a tea around 9.30 in the morning at office, he asked his wife for a cup of tea, only to get a rude shock, 'why ! just an hour back you had tea with breakfast, frequently having tea is not good at this age.'

Ranganathan thought, since he is retired he can have a nap in the afternoon, but then he remembered he has to give tuition to his grandson.

During lunch his wife gave him another surprise,'tomorrow before the maid comes we will have to clean all the ceiling fans, it was cleaned last Diwali, last time I could get Ramu for cleaning the same with great difficulty now when ever I call him he is avoiding me', Ranganathan told her, 'you may not be giving him enough money', his wife retorted back, 'why should we give money unnecessarry, now since you do not have to go to office, you can do it.' Ranganathan did not protest, silently went to his room after lunch.

His wife shown him where to find tea, sugar and milk to make the afternoon tea as she can visit her friend now she need not worry, all these years she sacrificed her own likings, it is good someone is at home when Malay comes from school.

It was past 4.30 pm a group of people came home, they wanted some donation for an old age home which was underway initiated by some youth group. Ranganathan argued with them, why do you seek donation from retired people like us? It is the responsibility of the children to look after their parents; they should not be shunted to old age homes, when they need the comfort of loved ones. The leader of this wing told him, 'uncle on retirement you got a handsome amount as gratuity and provident fund, over and above you are getting pension from the government, why don't you share some amount for the benefit of the miserable old people of your age. Ranganathan came up with a cheque of rupees one thousand, which they refused as the minimum standard they fixed was rupees five thousand.

After a month of boring life, Ranganathan tried to get a job with a private company, they called him, selected him but they were not ready to pay him the salary as per their job requirement, they simply said you are getting handsome pension every month then why you are asking so much salary, there are plenty of youngsters ready for this job, why we should not recruit them ! Ranganathan was surprised at their statement but he did not argue with them, this is the mind set, Let God save them from such notion.

Ranganathan thought he missed the wonderful time he had in the office, at any time he can get tea by pressing the call bell, today he will have to prepare the tea himself. He already has some jobs on hand; dusting the ceiling fans, calling the plumber to attend the leaking tap, the fan in the store room is out of order, polishing of the furniture, the cleaning of the over head tank. His wife used to tell him you could have learned some plumbing and electrical work during your leisure time, these things are costing us a lot, now since you are free, if you can do these things we will be saving a lot.

He had planned that he will spend time with his wife, he will take his wife to places they have not seen, but the hard reality is that he has to now adjust to new set of rules for himself, all his life he lived for others working in a company, now after retirement he has to work for the same people at home, what an irony?

He knew his wife has remarkably done well all these years, without taking a break or making a complaint, she is only seeking some assistance from him, as he is retired and available now.

Malay came from the next room,'grand pa, I want to go to the park to play with my friends, but mummy has asked me to finish the homework with you.'

Oh ! Ranganathan thought,' I am still a milking cow.'

18. Railway Platform.

Paresh was waiting at the Railway station to receive his uncle and family. The Platform was busting with activities. Among the passengers some had reservation, while at some counters people were waiting in long queues to get tickets. The refreshment counters were crowded, there are varieties of food items; people will consume more than they need, there after show their displeasure; it is an opportunity to eat anything and everything at your disposal. You know it is junk food but still one goes for it.

Paresh settled on an empty steel chair. He was cursing the railway for not providing comfortable seating as the new steel chairs are not at all comfortable. You slide down slowly , every minute you have to raise yourself to sit upright. The train for which he was waiting was almost an hour late.

A fat lady with her children occupied the seat next to him, she was complaining about the overcrowded waiting room. She was stuffing the things which she must have purchased while coming to the railway station into a tiny bag. It was a desperate attempt as the tiny bag could not take any more. It is a practice a habit in India to over stuff your bag with things. Paresh was wondering if she would continue packing and repacking even after boarding the train. Though the railway has placed bins at various points some passengers still throw the disposable glasses on the track as is the habit.

Hats off to the railways for managing and diverting large number of trains to all destinations, a really tough task as this being the largest net work of trains in the world. It is expected of the passengers to co operate with the railways.

Paresh got up from his seat, he moved, walked up and down on the crowded platform to straighten up. Once again there was an announcement that the train he was waiting is further delayed by half an hour. Paresh talked himself "When ever we wish to travel or wait for someone the train will be always late".

A large board was displayed on a high raised structure which read, 'Abolish child labour encourage them to attend school; their place is in the school.' Paresh was wondering, it is a distant dream of India. There are cases when a child is forced to earn lively hood, without looking in to the circumstances which is forcing them to work. The government is issuing orders and putting up huge banners.

Look at the quality of schools run by the government in the villages, the drop out ratio is very high because of non availability of high school education in the villages.

The railway police arrested some boys, who were hardly fifteen years old, engaged in menial work. The people though busy to catch their train will not pass without registering their comments, "These boys will enter the compartments for cleaning the floor and get away with the things they can lay their hands escaping the attention of passengers". Paresh thought people have lost their sensitivity, nobody has the time to look in to the circumstances which forces them to do this.

Paresh again found an empty seat near an old man. He too was waiting for the same train to arrive. The old man was holding a news paper, he said, "The time has changed; the quality of news getting deteriorated day by day. Now-a-days it is full of accidents, rapes and suicide. Sometimes I am scarred to open the news paper in the morning; the news is always very disturbing, the world has changed drastically; there don't seem to be an end to all these."

Paresh agreed with the old man they continued their discussion. The old man introduced himself as Bharat Raval, his son is working with Reliance Company, Ramesh Raval his son is known to Paresh, though they are not directly connected by work, as they are in different departments.

Paresh said he was waiting for this train as his uncle and family is joining them, he will see them after several years, as he was in Australia for almost a decade.

The coolies are a rare sight at the platforms with the introduction of wheeled bags and suitcase; it is a revolution, we can only spot coolies at major stations. Bharat Raval narrated , 'we never thought in our wildest dream that one day we will have to pay for the drinking water, that too in bottles.'

Finally the announcement was loud on the microphone in three languages; the train will reach in a few minutes.

Paresh positioned himself where the indicator mentioned B2 coach,most of the passengers were getting down here,he was eagerly waiting to spot his uncle;he had to wait longer as passengers were getting down slowly, this being a junction it is sure the train will halt for fifteen minutes ; so no worries.

His uncle and aunty got down with Sneha and Sunil, Paresh greeted them and looked for a coolie, but it was not needed as they were carrying very light luggage, they pushed forward through the crowded platform towards the exit. His uncle looked back as someone shouted, 'Girish ! wait I am coming,Girish put down his bag and ran back to Bharat Raval his old friend, they embraced each other,Girish's wife also rushed in,it was an emotional moment, they all exchanged greetings, they were old friends, they studied in the same school and college, they were living in the same locality years back.Though they met each other after a long time; they were always in contact with each other. Paresh mentioned,'My self and uncle were waiting at the platform without knowing that both of us were waiting for the same person.'

Now there was a tussle between Paresh and Bharat Raval, as with whom their guest will stay.

Girish finally declared that initially he will stay with Paresh and after the engagement of his daughter with Bharat's son; they will spend a couple of days with his childhood friend.

This childhood friendship has taken a new turn, the entire family got absorbed in the stories of Girish and Bharat, now they are relatives. It was a great moment to meet old friends, Bharat had invited many of their old friends for the engagement, it was a great meeting place.

After the engagement all of them again assembled at the same railway station, Girish and family was travelling back with refreshed old memories.

This railway platform has no leisure time, it is busy all the time, it never rests or sleeps, always live, serving the people, leading them to all directions and destination, feeding them, nursing them, giving them moments to remember, a never ending moment a never ending journey, wishing all the passengers a safe and happy journey.

19. Sky is the limit.

Pranlal is a self made man, he is originally from Rajasthan. He left his home under extreme circumstances. He was the eldest in the family of a sister and two brothers. He came in search of job to Ahmedabad in the seventies.

His family at far off village called Barmer in Rajasthan was practically starving. His parents were bonded labourers. Both of them died due to ill health leaving their children at the mercy of the land lord. The children were again engaged by the land lord to repay the loans taken by their parents; they too were working at the farm.

Pranlal was the eldest, he was sixteen years old. He studied only till fifth standard; thereafter helping his parents in repaying the loan by working with them. One night after the dinner he choked out a plan with his brother and sister to escape from the captivity of the land lord. He told them we will have to leave this village and work elsewhere otherwise we too will end up like our parents.

An elderly man working as a watchman looking after the godown and the servant's quarters, always had a soft corner for these children. When Pranlal approached him for his help he was very happy to support them, he allowed them to runaway advising them never to return to this village. He told them "don't worry you escape from here, I will handle the issue". He gave them some cash, "Keep this money. It will be handy for you, don't bother to give it back".

"Cha-cha (uncle) we are indebted to you for helping us run off and the cash you have given us; we will come back one day to this village".The old man nodded and waved them goodbye.

All the three got in to the train in an unreserved compartment, which headed for Ahmedabad. They got down at the station, crossed the platform, reached a dead end from where they found an exit, opening at a long series of slums.

They were approached by a youth Dhiren of around the same age of Pranlal. Some sort of telepathy worked between these two; within no time they were friends. Pranlal thanked God for protecting his sister and brother; as they took a wild risk for escape and freedom. Their struggle just started in this city of opportunities. They settled at the end of the slum occupied by an old lady living solely by begging, she now got a family. Pranlal thanked Dhiren for this kind gesture and asked him to find a job for him.

Pranlal went with Dhiren and hired a hand cart on daily basis to transport the goods to a warehouse owned by a business man. He left his sister with the old lady. He asked the old lady not to go for begging; he assured her that he will take care of all her needs, the old lady Jasoda was very happy to get the company of these loving children. Jasoda's entire family was wiped out in the devastating flood at Morvi town, she lost everything, followed by this tragedy she lost her mental balance. She was in a mental hospital for some time; later on she was discharged from the hospital. She had no place to go, that's how she reached here. She thanked God for sending these loving children to take care of her at this old age.

Pranlal's brother Rohit was going to a tea stall to earn his daily wages. He toiled and worked hard to earn a good amount to feed the family of four. His sister was 12 years old and was helping Jasoda in the house hold work.

Pranlal's employer was in the business of intermediate dyes used by the textile units, he was pulling the cart to shift the rejected material from the warehouse to another godown which will be again loaded in the tractors to be shifted to plant for reprocessing.

Pranlal made suggestion to get a temporary shed near the plant so that they can save the daily trip of tractors carrying the rejected materials to the plant.

The employer was very much impressed by this cost saving suggestion. In recognition of his suggestion, sincereity and hard work, he was promoted as supervisor. He was a quick learner; his employer was highly satisfied with his work and offered him a small accommodation inside the premises where all of them shifted.

Pranlal knew he has to make it fast, he cannot afford to waste time, in order to achieve his dream he will require certain basic education. So all of them joined night classes to educate themselves. Pranlal cleared his school final exam; this boosted his confidence.

Old lady Jasoda was very happy with these children; who took care of her very well. She considered them as her own children, she thanked God, she had no more complaints in life.

Pranlal's brother started his own tea stall, he is earning good income, his sister Santok completed her school final exams and got married to Dhiren. He was very helpful when they came to Ahmedabad. Dhiren is staying with them as he has no one in his family.

Earning a livelihood is not the aim of Pranlal. He has seen poverty, the miserable condition of his parents as bonded labourers. He along with his brother and sister faced the wrath of the land lord, he was determined to make a mark for himself.

The employer found a never ending energy level in Pranlal, he was taking lot of interest in the factory activities, he took interest in the production line, he mastered and aquired practical knowledge of running the plant. He enrolled for evening Diploma in engineering, which he completed. He was now looking after the plant's engineering division, a work which he performed efficiently.

Pranlal asked Dhiren to go to his village and procure as much land as he can, at whatever price it is available; he covered a lot of ground. The villagers never knew who the original owner of the land was as the lands were in the control of the land lord. Dhiren approached the land lord, offered him more than what he can get in the next fifty years for this barren land. He was tempted by the high price he was offered. A deal was made and both parted smiling at each other; only time will tell who had the advantage.

The old lady Jasoda fell sick, the entire family took care of her. Before breathing her last she called all of them and handed over an old torn bag with bundles of currency notes and said "all of you took care of me when I needed you the most, you are my children, I was waiting for a right moment to hand over this to you before I say final good bye, I do not know how much is in there. This is the amount I have collected by begging. I wish you all a bright life, live in peace and harmony". Old lady Jasoda passed away. Pranlal performed the last rites. After the mourning period was over all of them assembled and counted the bundle. There was close to seven lac rupees (seven hundred thousand) in it. They were surprised. How could anyone have accumulated such a huge sum by begging? Unbelievable!!

They decided they will not touch this amount for their personal requirement but will form a trust in the name of Jasodamata and help the needy from the interest of this amount.

'Good culture and good thoughts are always associated with morality, an education without morality is of no use.'

Pranlal went ahead with his plan to set up a dyes plant in his home town. He submitted the project to the government, he got the necessary sanction and clearance including the required loan for this project.

All of them visited the village in the new luxury car they purchased, met all the villagers, old friends of their parents, arranged a feast, invited the entire villagers including the land lord, it was a celebration, they gifted elders each of them with a pair of dress.

The land lord met them, he was very old now, he narrated his problem, his son only knows to spend he is not capable of generating any wealth, he is good for nothing. He told them he is suffering because of his greediness and unethical dealings, he hoped God will forgive him.

Pranlal had only sympathy for him, it is only because of the land lord he is self sufficient today. Without uttering any harsh words to the land lord he listened to him patiently. He promised to extend all help whenever he needed it.

After the departure of the land lord, Pranlal told his brother and sister,"We have the greatest weapon at our disposal, forgiveness, let us forgive him, It is because of him we are on this progressive path, he is only instrumental in the sequence of events".

Pranlal along with Dhiren, Santok and Rohit made a surprise visit to the old cha-cha (uncle). He was very old with poor vision, his memory was very sharp. He recognised Pranlal.They all thanked him for the kind gesture, took his blessings. He was invited to light the lamp on the foundation laying ceremony of their factory.

The factory was set up and started its production, it paved way for employment to thousands of villagers, a small time bonded labourer showed the way to the world,

'There is nothing one cannot achieve with determination and drive.
There is no substitute for hard work, only sky is the limit.'

20. Torch bearer.

Hargovind is a reformist coming from a backward region of Uttar Pradesh. He made several representations to various political and non-political organisations to improve the conditions of the government schools.

He is worried about the increasing number of private schools. He tried to prove a point by objecting the private schools and their heavy fees, which is beyond the reach of common middle class parents. The parents are stretching beyond their capacity for the education of their children, that is the reason he is demanding for corrective actions to improve the standard and quality of the government run schools.

The Rotary club was conducting a youth festival for all the district schools, some schools were serious participants where as some schools sent their entries without any preparation.

Hargovind is determined to show the strength against the might of private schools. He is the principal of a government run school. He found the best among students without any bias to train and prepare them for the youth festival.

Just two kilometers from this government school is situated the private school run by a sitting MLA. It is a modern school with all amenities and comfort.

The Modern School, is a residential school with all the facilities. The class rooms are air-conditioned, different play grounds for football, hockey and cricket. An indoor and outdoor badminton court, basket ball court, grounds for track and field events, swimming pool and what not.

They charged very high fees which only certain class can afford. The school is famous but getting admission there is very difficult. The trustees have difficulty dealing with influential people.

The school had well trained staff, experts in their subjects; there were residential teachers as well as local teachers from the city.

The principal is a lady in her fifties. She is a retired defence person and a tough task master. She will not spare even the staff if they make any mistake. When a student scores low marks she will summone the teachers and demand an explanation for the deteriorating standard of the student, in short she wanted accountability on all matters.

The youth festival for all the district schools were conducted by the Rotary club. The judges assembled for the extempore speech competition for the 14 to 16 age group. It was quite interesting. The students were given subject on the spot by draw system. They had to pick up a chit and speak on the subject instantly for five minutes.

This is a very useful and interesting event for the students, as it revealed the knowledge update on the current topics.

Some students would come to the stage, pick up a chit, wait a while and without speaking a word, go back to their seat. Some stumbledd and repeated the subject given to them. It was fun but a pity of our education system that the students were unable to apply their mind.

The five judge panel will share their views and declare the winner. Shabana a psychiatrist by profession was among the panel of judges, others were all from the Rotary club holding high positions in business and industries.

There were two prominent schools, going neck to neck in the competition.

The Modern school and the government run school. It is a pity the government school do not have sufficient teaching staff, they do have a common play ground, but not enough fund for sports equipments. Their staff is well qualified, they encourage students in their overall personality development. The principal Hargovind used to mingle freely with the students to get back certain feed backs on teaching and other problems faced by the students.

The tough competition was with the girl from Government school and the boy from the residential school.

After the extempore speech the chief judge declared the result, it went in favour of the girl from the government school.

On his concluding speech the Rotarian mentioned, "Intelligence is God's gift. Training and coaching can be given but finally it is one's intelligence which emerges as a winner." He also mentioned a very small percentage of students are interested in sports.

We can take the horse to the pond; but we cannot force it to drink water.

Shabana the psychiatrist emphasised the need for reforms in the field of education. She mentioned, in every class of fifty students only top five students are cream, followed by next ten students in the range of first class, another twenty to twenty five students falls under average, the rest is not serious in studies, not that they are not capable of doing better, but they are the neglected lot by the schools.

She was concerned about the increasing suicide rates among the students because of the stress of education, from both schools and parents.

Lack of motivation, over stress due to competition, lengthy syllabus, irrelevant subjects all contribute in the deterioration of educational standard.

The students good in sports are looked down upon by the teachers in particular.

She narrated an incident, "I was taking a class to measure and analyse the initiative and drive among the students of a well reputed school. The boy who was in the ninth standard was sitting as dumb as a statue. I observed him for two weeks. I met the teachers and his parents with the boy sitting next to them. To my surprise I found that this happened only recently otherwise he was very good at sports and quite active in the class."

One day I noticed this boy was going in the opposite direction of the school, I followed him, he went to the bushes adjacent to a deserted park. On reaching him I saw he swallowed something, he panicked when I approached him, I saw a bottle on the side, he was rushed to the hospital, called the parents, informed the school authorities all of them rushed to the hospital. His mother was weeping. He was saved since he was rushed to the hospital in time.

The doctors advised complete rest for one week; but the question is will he be alright mentally, unless we remove the doubts bothering him, at this tender age if he has taken this extreme step; there is something wrong with our system.'

A retired judge who was the chief guest, stressed the need for improving the standard of government run schools, this will encourage the parents to send their children to such schools instead of sending them to private schools. A middle class parent stretches beyond their capacity to provide education to their children. The education is commercialised to such an extent that even the parents are also worried to meet the high demands of the school. The parents are equally stressed to meet the high tuition fees. This has effect on the children, at work place.

The key word is educational reforms with quality education, the task to improve the standard of government schools.

During thanksgiving, the Secretary passed a very vital remark, "Hope whatever is discussed here will not go waste. It should reach the HRD ministry, they must chalk out a definite plan to improve the conditions of all the government schools. It should not end like the vote bank politics. People like Hargovind are the torch bearer of such movement for reforms. The politicians should be accountable to their constituency, they must deliver, mere lip service will not do". Finaly he thanked all those who gathered there.

'There is light at the end of the tunnel.'

21. Ketul and Savita.

Savita was waiting for Ketul. He promised to meet her at the highway point from where it would be easy to get transportation to any direction they plan. Ketul asked her to bring two pairs of dress and nothing else.

Time is running out, Savita is worried as to why Ketul has not turned up. Ketul was her customer for quite a while. He visited her regularly, mostly during the weekends. He raised new hopes and dreams in her life.

She was one of those unfortunate, living in the red light area. There were many among her collegues who adjusted themselves, as there was no way out. During her early childhood she lost her parents. She was brought up by a distant uncle. She fell in love with a neighbour boy, Mithun. One fine day she eloped with him to the dream city Mumbai. Their joy was short lived; they were put up in a cheap dingy hotel. The main income of the hotel was on hourly basis, people came here with women for enjoyment.

Mithun went out to get some snacks; but he never returned. She never knew what happened to him. She was pennyless. On finding that she was deserted here by her boy friend, the hotel manager took advantage of the situation. She was offered a cold drink with laced substance which made her numb and he raped her. Savita was helpless. She cannot go back to her uncle. Later on under the pretext of giving her a job, a close aide of the hotel manager took her to the brothel.

Savita remembers the tough initial days, circumstances forced her in to this proffession. Most of the girls living there had similar stories to tell. They all were victims of unfortunate circumstances. In most of the cases they were here because of men and women who forced them in to this trade.The life in a brothel is different. The freedom is restricted, one who brings business is the favourite of the lady in charge living on the income generated by these girls. They are given new names when they enter in to the regular stream, they are supposed to forget their original names.

Savita looked at the watch tower, it was 5.00 pm, Ketul was supposed to be here by 4.30 pm. Her anxiety increased and she was scared and worried. Will she have to go back where she belonged !! the thought was haunting her.

She had not much information about Ketul, except that he was deeply in love with her. He wanted her to leave this profession, to get back to mainstream of life. He once told her that he is earning a handsome salary in a multinational company and his parents are living in Delhi.

The waiting reminded her of the painful experience she had undergone when she eloped with Mithun, landed in a God foresaken place. She was tired of this unfortunate life, she was thinking to end it. When she met Ketul, she hung to the straw of hope. She thought life has again shown mercy on her. She knew that the lady in charge would start hunting for her at all possible places, like bus stops, railway station and highways where she was waiting right now for Ketul. She was in double mind whether to go back or not.

Ketul was a different young man. His way of thinking, his approach to life and people were so different that sometimes his friends used to wonder: 'which world does he belong!!' He was very popular among his friends because of his helpful and loving nature.

None of his friends had any clue that he regularly visited a brothel for the past one year.

Past one year on his salary day, Ketul would spend his time with the destitute children or dine with a group of poor hungry beggars at an affordable restaurant. Sometimes he used to offer motorcycle rides to kids living in the slums with permission from their parents. In short he was a Robin Hood determined to bring some difference in the lives of the deprived misreables.

Once during a discussion among his friends over a news item on rehabilitation of girls rescued from the red light areas attracted his attention. They were rescued by a prominent NGO group. The girls were trained in different trades to earn a lively hood, some of them could not adjust to the new life style and went back to the hell were they came from. Rehabilitation of these girls are not easy. They should be given emotional and moral support. Years of troubled life cannot be converted in to smooth sailing. A social worker had appealed to the people to adopt these girls in to the mainstream, he said 'help them get back to life'. He also appealed the youth to come forward and marry these unfortunate girls to give them a new lease of life. They are in the brothels because of some evil forces.

There were protest against the social worker on his idea to bring the dirt back to the society. Some elders even asked for strong action against him for misleading the public and the youth. This was the time when Ketul took a firm stand that he will bring luck in the life of an unfortunate girl. He visited the brothel where he came accross Savita. He spent days together listening to her sorry past. Who does not have a past? But Savita's past was a miserable one. Ketul was determined to provide a bright future for savita.

"If we live in the sorrow it will never go; we have to bring happiness, try to find happiness to ward off the sorrows".

Ketul reached the spot in a car with some of his friends. They saw Savita silently walking among some people towards a stationery van. He had no other go than challenging them. Savita on seeing Ketul released herself from the cluthches of people around her. She ran towards Ketul like in a Bollywood movie. His friends cordoned both Ketul and Savita protecting them. Both were guided to get in to the car. In all likelyhood under such circumstances there would be a scuffle, but the people who came to get back Savita did not show the keenness to capture her back, it was clear from their expression that they allowed her to escape from this hell,though they were much more stronger than Ketul's army of friends.

They had the golden heart to release Savita. The society should appreciate people like Ketul in bringing change in the way of thinking, then the world will be a better place to live.

22. The loot.

The courtroom was full, all were eagerly waiting for the Judge to take his seat. It was a case of shooting an innocent man to death by the police. Sheth Dyanchand was sitting silently, his lawyers advising him as to what statement he should make in the court. Dyanchand had made up his mind. He thought it was his fault, he doubted the sincereity, faithfulness and integrity of Vikram which lead the police to take some action under certain circumstances, which resulted in the death of his loyalist Vikram Singh

Dyanchand can never pardon himself from this, he decided to take full responsibility of the killing of Vikram Singh.

Judge was yet to arrive; hence people were busy talking to each other. The court corridor was bustling with activities, full of lawyers, criminals, innocents, undertrials , but Dyanchand's mind was very much disturbed on the surface and deeply inwardly. He was in the prison of time, time being the past, time being the thought, he was in the prison of thought.

Down the memory lane he recollected Vikram Singh was employed as a security in charge with his business organisation under special circumstances.

One would normally find Vikram in plain clothes, he was a well built man with a height of six feet. He was in his forty's, his main brief was to be shadow to the man he was protecting. He was what you call a standout, you could make out he was made of tough stuff and he would easily stand out even in a crowd.

Vikram had already put in around 25 years of service with this group. It's an interesting story how he got to work with this business organisation.

Twenty five years ago, Dyanchand was a small-time business man, who mainly dealt textile products. During the initial days he had a lot of touring to do to develop his business, moving across cities along with his wares. One day after delivering an order in Surat, he decided to stay back for the night. This was against his normal practice, but that day he was exhausted, so he decided to look for a decent place to spend the night. Dyanchand was carrying cash with him which he got as payment for his goods. He had already sent the truck back to his hometown with the remaining goods. He was unaware that he was being followed by a team of thugs. They had been following him for quite some time now. Dyanchand got down from his auto and was heading towards his hotel, when suddenly from nowhere in the dark he was attacked with a heavy object. It was around midnight, there were hardly any people on the road. The attackers were after the bag that contained cash. One of the attackers took out a knife and threatened to use it on Dyanchand. They snatched the bag from his hand and were about to flee when from nowhere a young teenager came to the scene with a hockey stick in hand. He threw himself on them, the boy in no time over powered the drunken thugs and got the bag back, the gang fearing being caught by the police, ran away into the darkness of the night. The boy was hurt but fine.

Dyanchand thanked the boy, and asked him his name. The teenager introduced himself as Vikram singh. There was pride in his tone when he pronounced his name. Dyanchand asked the boy, "do you know how much cash is in this bag?" Pat came the reply, "Seth, whatever is the amount it can't be more valuable than your life".

Dyanchand was impressed by the answer given by this young lad, Dyanchand asked him what he did for a living and the young lad replied he would take up any odd job just to ensure he could have enough money to have two square meals a day. That day onwards Vikram singh never had to worry about where his next meal would come from and Dyanchand would always remain Seth sahib for Vikram.

For the next twenty five years, Vikram was joined to his hip. Wherever Dyanchand went he followed. Night time when even the shadow would betray Seth, Vikram would be with him. Every important business transaction and deal would have Vikram's steely gaze on it. Since that fateful night in Surat. Dyanchand expanded and diversified his business. Apart from his other ventures Dyanchand also got into mining. Mining was new to him, wherein he had to deal with hardened labour force. He used to interact with his work force on a weekly basis as this business was a profitable one for him and he wanted to have a tight grip on things. Meanwhile Vikram remained the only constant in his life. He had appointed a staff to look after the affairs of the mines and the miners.

Every month the payout to the workers was around rupees fifty lacs (five millions) and the responsibility to ensure the pay reached on time to the mine's office was that of Vikram and a head clerk from the firm. With changing times there were suggestions that every worker should have his own bank account and that his salary be electronically deposited there. But somehow that never got materialized. The illiterate work force preferred getting cash in hand.

Pay day was the only day when Vikram would not be by the side of his Seth. He would leave office early with the mini cash trunk with the salaries in it in his station wagon along with two other staff members. Vikram always made it a point to start early as the mines were around 250 kms from the office. He was aware of how eagerly his arrival was awaited by the labour force. He was like a Messiah for them. One ill fated day he was accompanied as usual by the salary clerk and the driver. They were supposed to reach after noon, but got delayed by an engine failure in the vehicle. Finally after the driver and Vikram got their hands dirty with grease they proceed towards the mines. It was well pass sunset. He came across a road block and noticed a diversion symbol suggesting they take that route.

Vikram Singh was upset that nothing was going as planned. However the delay only made him extra alert and cautious. Something seemed to bother him and when they had to pass a tunnel his intuition told him that there was some foul play somewhere. His worst fears came true, after entering the tunnel he saw half a dozen men blocking the way. Sensing the danger he asked the driver to switch off the head lights and put the vehicle in reverse gear. He told the two men with him in the station wagon that he would be getting down with the trunk, as the men blocking the path were behind the cash. Vikram jumped from the vehicle along with the trunk and disappeared taking advantage of the darkness. The miscreants were seasoned enough to overpower the station wagon and within no time they were on the trail of Viram's path. Early in the morning the driver and clerk managed to find their way back to the office. By now everyone had their own theories. Stories were flying thick and fast. Not for even a single moment did Dyanchand doubt his trusted aide Vikram. When most of them had their accusatory finger pointed at Vikram, the seth reminded them that Vikram was made of different stuff.

It was now two days since the incident, there is no clue of Vikram, the money or of the people who were chasing him. Rupees fifty lac (five million) was a huge amount and by the 3rd day the police got involved. After questioning the driver and clerk, police turned to Dyanchand and asked him to provide them with a recent photograph of Vikram.They also wanted a detailed list of employees working at the mines and asked if there were any notorious guys amongst them.

Police got down to business; they activated their network of informers and started questioning habitual offenders.They rounded up suspects from the area.They also visited the mining site and also the route Vikram took; they questioned the staff over there as well.They went through the list extensively and kept a watch on a certain group of men.

It was found that some of them for the past one week regularly after their dinner assembled at an abandoned old broken shed which was at times used to house temporary employees of the mines.

Time was running out, and Seth Dyanchand was summoned by the police to update him with the investigation.They seeded doubt into Dyanchands mind, he now realised that, he was all these years underpaying Vikram and that rupees ten thousand was very less compared to the hours he put in and the rising prices.He finally filed an official complaint and named Vikram in it.

With an FIR naming him the hunt was on for Vikram. Police had intensified their search and extended their search area to nearby villages.

Vikram Singh's captivators were waiting for the right time to finish him off and escape with the bag. They were aware that any misjudgement from them and the police would turn the heat on them. They had beaten him blue, chained him and deprived him of food and water. All this while the group had time only to booze and count the cash. They knew that this cash was enough to change their life.

Vikram occasionally gained conciousness, but he was too weak to even move. He wasn't aware of the location where they had kept him. All this while he was planning as to how he could free himself and flee from his captors and save his Seth's money. He noticed that the escape vehicle was ready; the goons had a new jeep ready for that purpose.

At the far end of the hall he was tied down. He could see that the cash had already been transferred to another bag and the trunk was left empty. He saw all the five of his captors were drunk; this was his chance. He knew if he could somehow manage to untie himself, he could take on these goons and run with the money. He stretched his legs with the last ounce of strength at his disposal he managed to get a metal object near to his tied arm. For the next hour he worked on cutting the rope. Finally his hands were free. Without alerting his captors he had managed to untangle his legs too. He crawled and hid behind a pillar on the darkest part of the room. All this while Vikram had only seen five men, he was taken aback when he spotted the sixth man in the room. He was the driver who rode along with Vikram that fateful day. Vikram soon connected the dots. He realised that it was an insider's job.

The only thing in his mind was that he had to get his master's money to the rightful hands. He was certain that once the police would get the clue about the driver, they would apprehend everyone behind this and they would take the case to its logical end.

The men under heavy influence of alcohol weren't aware of Vikram's moves. He sneaked closer to the bag, wasted no time in putting it on his shoulders and dashed towards the bikes parkedoutside. He then realised that the keys of the bike were on the table near the party, he went back to get the key. He didn't start the bike fearing it would alert the half conscious captors, so he dragged the bike till some distance and then started the engine. One kick, the bike was on top gear.

He zoomed past the road as a man possessed he knew his condition and that he could lose consciousness anytime. He wanted to reach the office before he passed out again. At a distance he saw a barricade; his heart skipped a beat. He raced towards it. He could see seth Dyanchand's car along with the police patrol vehicle. As he approached the barricade a shot was fired aiming at Vikram from the service revolver of Police Inspector which hit Vikram in the chest.

Vikram crashed along with the bike against the barricade. While giving his dying declaration to the police he was staring at his Seth. He gave all the necessary information to the cops, he looked at his Seth one last time. With his dying breath he tried to salute his master one last time. His raised hands were dropped by his side.

Sitting at the court Dyanchand was cursing himself, for he knew he had committed a sin. He Killed his most trusted employee, who stood by his side for the past twenty five years. He had made a mistake by doubting Vikram. He decided he would ask for the harshest punishment from the courts for doubting brave and loyal Vikram. His complaint led the police to fire a shot in order to arrest him.

Vikram's last attempt to salute his master was repeatedly haunting Seth Dyanchand. It will continue to disturb him rest of his life.

23. Time Pass.

Kalyani was working at the bank as an officer. She was very efficient in her job. She had the knack of getting the work done. She was what you call street smart. She was so smart that at times she even made her Boss to finish her work.

Kalyani had a different approach to life. She was equally popular among her female as well as male colleagues at the bank. She was a happy go lucky person. She knew she wasn't as good looking as many others who worked with her, but she balances it up with her charm and wit.

She had a good fashion sense and she did justice to all kinds of outfits. I was a peon with the bank but her mannerisms were such that she always put me at ease whenever we interacted.

The bank's previous manager was a man with strong work ethics and was in every sense strict. He ran a tight unit; he would come down hard on employees committing mistakes. Nevertheless he was well respected and popular with the staff because of this trait of his.

The new manager, Rajender was relatively new for this job profile. He is two months old into his new job role. He is in his forties, was endeauring and helpful by nature. He is father of two kids whom he could not bring along with him as they were in between their academic session so he deemed it right not to disturb them in the middle of their session. Untill the vacation he is a forced bachelor.

Kalyani was in her thirties married to a class-I government officer working else where. Both of them could not settle down at one place as they were placed in different cities with different organisations. Another reason for her reluctance to relocate was because this job was a well paying one. They decided to wait for some more time before both were in a position to work in the same city. This wait had already taken 2 years of separation.

Kalyani stayed in the Bank colony; Rajender meanwhile had to wait for some more time to get his designated apartment as the previous manager was yet to vacate the premises because he too was waiting for the academic year of his sons to get over.

I along with other bank work was assigned to bring lunch for Rajender sir from a near by restaurant. One day during the lunch break Kalyani approached her new manager and asked if she could join him at the table. She opened up her aromatic tiffin and offered Rajender very inviting looking koftas. He could not refuse the offer, it was just the way his mother used to prepare. He asked her how she could manage all the cooking so early in the morning and then be on time for work.

This sharing of lunch became a daily routine. There were times when Kalyani would not get her lunch, but would share food with what her boss used to get from the restaurant. She was this way with the rest of the staff as well. Within no time their friendship bloomed and gossip about them spread across the office. A senior by the name Manohar who was to retire soon would at times pass sarcastic remarks.

Within no time Rajender was smitten by Kalyani's charm and was head over heels in love with her. Once as I was returning back home from work I saw them both enter a movie hall. They were spotted by many going for shopping at near by malls. When ever Rajender had to buy something for his wife Ramila it used to be Kalyani's choice that would get billed. He said, 'Ramila will be always in sarees, I have a number of times asked her to try Punjabi dress or jeans but she is very simple in dressings; she will tell me our children are growing; it is time for them to wear fashionable dress, this time I am going to surprise her.'

Rajender was to leave for a few days to be with his family. Kalyani asked to give her regards to his wife and kids and said she was very happy to see him loving them so much. Rajender was quick to realise that the topic wasn't going in the desired direction. When they reached the mall he bought her a very costly party outfit for her, in return she got a decent shirt for him. Dinner at a chic new restaurant followed.

Rajender by now had showered Kalyani with many expensive gifts and most of the time the two were seen in the company of each other.

One day Manohar in good faith confronted Rajender who was many years younger to him. He cautioned Rajender and asked him to gaurd himself as well as the position he holds against gossip's flying thick and fast in the office. He asked him not to get carried away by the modern ways of Kalyani. Manohar also asked him to uphold the prestige of the high office he was holding. Manohar was of the view if Rajender didn't check his ways things would get out of hand and in turn it would wreck his married life. Rajender came to know that the entire office was cooking up stories about them behind their backs.

Rajender did not react to Manohar, he respected him because of his age, and deep down there was some truth in what manohar had said.

Soon Rajender started finding faults in his wife, he forgot the fact that she was single handedly taking care of their children. Love is blind and he started shrinking away from his responsibility towards his family. He went to the extend of asking Kalyani to seek divorce from her husband, and assured her that he would also send his wife a divorce notice.

Now Rajender started forcing her to get separated from her husband. She at times avoided the topic. She asked him what was wrong with the current arrangement. She believed that one should try and enjoy the present and that for her being married or divorced was just for the society and she didn't attach any importance to that status.

Their story wasn't going anywhere because for her view of life, but it certainly reached the head office. This was a tricky situation for the top management to look into. They were grown up, educated and good at their work.

During a meeting he attended at the head office, Rajender was advised by the divisional head to ensure that rumours were laid to rest and that the bank could not afford any negative publicity or disrepute. Rajender assured his boss that he would ensure that the bank name wasn't sullied and that work would not be affected in any manner.

Next day when he reached the Bank he found a leave application from Kalyani on his desk. She was taking leave for two days. After the two days she didn't report to work for two more days, she had extended her leave. Rajender was furious and this also affected his work.

On the fifth day she came to the office. She had got a box of sweets along with her she distribute the same to the office staff. She was in a happy mood, her husband Manoj had secured a transfer to the city would be joining her in a week's time. She even thrust a sweet piece in to Rajender's mouth, this was unexpected. He painfully congratulated her. The atmosphere completely changed in the office. The office staff gathered around her to study her face, but she was at her usual jovial best. People were looking for signs of disappointment but she showed none.

The only person who seemed to be upset about the news was Rajender. He was in no man's land, trying hard to control his emotions. He felt as if he was just another character in the play. He contemplated what he could do to get out of this embarrassing situation, all thoughts were inclining towards him taking a transfer else where, as it would at least be a face saver.

24. The ungrateful me.

It was Palanpur (Gujarat). I remember our house surrounded by plenty of banyan trees, with trunks touching the ground. Monkey's paradise, it was a beautiful sight, little monkey's clutching to the stomach of mother monkeys, jumping from one branch to another, sliding down fast, pick up something from the tree or the ground and eat, snatching biscuits from my hand, a lot of them having their night halt on the branches. Later in my life I found out that monkeys never make homes; though they have families, they jump from one branch to the other, from one tree to the other, move towards the jungle for safety. Their unsteadiness is compared with the human mind by philosophers.

Back home at Narakkal in Kerala we had a large number of trees in our compound, the coconut, beatle nuts, mangoes, jack fruits and many varieties. We have plucked the tender mangoes from the tree during the season.

I played with my friends on these mangoe trees by tieing ropes from one branch to the other by making swings to play, it has given us plenty of mangoes. We never bother once our requirement was over, we never thank them.

At the age of ten I moved to Mithapur (Gujarat), we had a fairly large compound with two badam trees, one neem tree and two coconut trees, apart from the other plants.

Kids and grownups all like badam, which had a typical taste, difficult to explain. The neem tree was just at the corner of the boundary wall, the high school play ground was clearly visible from here.

The branches of badam trees were close to the neem tree. The natural branching of the neem tree made a comfortable shape to make a tree house.

The badam tree offered me some of its branches to fullfil my dream house. I placed those badam branches on the triangular formation of neem tree branches, tied them placed thick gunny bags. Covered all the three sides and the top with gunny bags. It measured roughly a height of 5 to 6 feet. The front opened at the high school play ground.

This tree house was comfortable for three persons. We climb up the tree house to watch the inter-departmental cricket match during Sundays. We pluck badam from the tree or get hot homemade snacks from the kitchen and enjoy the match. It was an ashiana self made for fun and enjoyment.

Back at Ernakulam in Kerala, there too we had plenty of fruits, vegetables and trees. Prominent was the jackfruit tree and the mango tree. From our terrace we could pluck the mangoes. We had a hooked stick made of bamboo to easily pluck the mangoes. Sometimes we get the left over mangoes picked on by birds.

We have enjoyed the fruits, the coolness of its shade, the branches to make swings to play. The trees have entertained us whatever we demanded from it without any protest. I never realised we were getting all these for free. We could not understand the language of these trees. They are like caretakers to all of us. They never scolded us, instead welcomed us by spreading their branches, took us in to its core, and allowed us to enjoy every bit of it.

Never even once I realised and bothered to look back; every time I moved from one place to another they were there to welcome extending all the comforts with fruits, shade and the tender coconut water of high energy.

During my childhood I made use of everything offered to me by these trees, I drifted as and when I started growing, a time came I was completely away from their wonderful company, I do not remember when I was totally cut off, how can I be so selfish!! But I was selfish,I was busy elsewhere doing different things, away from nature and its love.

One day I visited my cousins at Narakkal in Kerala, we visited our grandparent's old place, the house was no more, it was demolished, what existed was a flat land, most of the old trees I recognised; they too must have recognised me; I felt as if they were telling me, 'where were you all these years, come let us play, I am old now, hope you will stay back with us.'

I touched the parental figure; I was feeling shy to hug them in front of my cousins, still escaping their attention I took them in my open arms, it gave me great satisfaction, my eyes were wet; I controlled my tears; I abandoned them when they really need me, the branches were old and weak, I did not look back, I went back with a heavy heart.

At Ernakulam in Kerala which was home to us for almost more than 4 decades, was disposed by my parents; it is owned by some one else now. During one of our visit to this place, myself and my brother asked the taxi driver to drive slowly as we wanted to have a glimpse of the old place. The house was as it was, same colour, the mango tree was very much there with mangoes on it. We did not stop there: we just passed but the glimpses of the tree reminded and brought back many memories of the past.

After retirement from the work I had the good opportunity to visit back Mithapur (Gujarat). I asked a friend to take me round the place I played.

It gave me shock to see the two badam trees, the coconut trees and the neem tree missing. The tree house which was our entertainment centre was no more there.

When we grow how conveniently we forget the contribution of nature and environment in our upbringing. We neglect those which once entertained us, played with us, fed us with delicious fruits, provide us with cool shade during summer, many of us sleep under the shade of these trees which protect us from heat, provide us with cool air. We do not bother to protect them when they need us.

'How could I be so ungrateful?'

25. Remand.

The investigation officer came heavily on the murder accused who was brought by the city police force. They nabbed him from his home. His name they said is Quereshi, a rickshaw driver.

A city businessman was murdered while returning from office. The CCTV footage was not very clear, but resembled the culprit who was now in custody.

The pressure was mounting on the police department from chamber of commerce, the legislative members to get a breakthrough in this case.

The media was highlighting and tracking the case since almost after a week the police failed to come out with any leads.

Now they got the breakthrough from the CCTV footage, they were questioning him. It is almost three days now, but the accused refused to all their questions. He said he was not in the city during that day. His rickshaw was not on the road. He had gone to Ajmer to see his uncle who was hospitalized.

The police was not ready to listen to his story. It was identified and confirmed as he resembled the CCTV footage picture, but it was not clear, there seemed a slight resemblance. It was found that he used to park his rickshaw just close to the victims office.

The investigation officer wanted to finish this matter as the pressure was mounting from the commissioner's office. He had to apply third degree method to extract the truth. The accused was tortured to spell out what the police dictated.

Quereshi was around forty years old, married, with two school going kids. He was continuously refusing, requesting the authorities about his innocence.The torture crossed the elastic limits, finally he could no more resist, agreed to what the police charged, the murder of this businessman.

The Officer signaled to stop, and ordered to dress him up. They declared to the media about this breaking news. All the channels were circulating this breaking news and achievement of the police department. Newspapers reported, "the police succeeded in solving a case without loosing much time."

Just when they were about to take Quereshi to the court, he suddenly freed himself from the guards, bounced and attacked the investigation officer, hit him on the head very hard with an iron rod, the officer died on the spot.

The police team were not ready for this sudden attack, they somehow managed to overpower Quereshi. Just then, another team of police reached the station with the actual murderer of the businessman.

It was too late when they reached with the breakthrough. The innocence of Quereshi was proved, but by that time he already became a murderer.

The pressure of investigation from all sides in a VIP's case on fastrack, takes toll of innocent people.

26. The hidden power of a woman.

Without a moments notice, Parvati's world suddenly crashed. It was as if the ground beneath her was turning into quicksand. She wasn't prepared for what life had in store for her. She is only 5 years into her marriage. She had everything she dreamed since childhood, a loving husband and two loving daughters.

She saw Karan and her neighbours approaching her with the news that Mahesh, her husband, was run over by a speeding truck. He was returning from work that fateful day. He was carrying balloons, toys, and sweets for his daughters, everything was lost.

The daughters could not understand what was happening, why was there such commotion and as to why their mummy was weeping nonstop, why wasn't their papa around, that's when the body arrived after postmortem. The entire neighborhood was feeling sorry for this family.

Parvati lost everything at one stroke, just this morning she had packed for him the lunch box, so she wasn't prepared for time to take away everything that was dear to her, her husband, her happiness, her small family!!

Time passed. The last rites were performed, most of the relatives left including her only brother who was running a small business in the neighboring town. She hoped her brother would stay back, he would support her, call her to come and stay with him, at least for a couple of months, but she soon learnt that life was miserable, time is supreme, time never waits for anyone, bad time could strike anytime as a thief and rob our happiness.

Parvati had nowhere to go, no one to turn to. The income stopped suddenly. There was no way she could scrape through a single day. She soon realized that it was up to her now to raise and educate her daughters. She is all they had.

Mahesh's friend Karan approached her, he got her to sign certain important papers which would help her in claiming some compensations. It came as a great relief for Parvati. She visualized God himself had come to her help in the form of Karan.

Karan had also approached Mahesh's employer and appraised them of the difficulties faced by the family after the accidental death. The employer was a kind hearted man, who agreed to give a job of a peon to Parvati as she had no formal education.

Time heals wounds, she started going to work. Slowly she adjusted to the new life, and she was determined to educate her daughters, so that they do not have to face the helplessness she was facing.

Parvati used to consult Karan on important matters and he used to extend all help to her family.

The evil once again raised it's ugly face. The villagers were now casting doubts about the relationship between Karan and Parvati. They started floating stories; even Karan's wife started believing the neighborhood stories and all hell broke loose.

Karan had to stop visiting the family only to spare Parvati from this ill campaign. The village elders labeled her as a loose character women .This disturbed the life of Parvati again. The family that was slowly trying to come to terms with reality of life was once again targeted. She lost the will to live. She thought about her kids, the thought of moving to another town also crossed her mind, but then where would she find a job in the new place. Time sometimes humiliates, bad time takes away all hope with it.

Back at work place the scenario changed. People were sympathetic to her till the other day, their opinions changed. The warmth and affection which was there till sometime back had disappeared; she found it difficult to continue.

In no time the attitude and behavior of the kind hearted employer changed. He called parvati to stay back one evening as he was expecting few guests in the office.

It was evening time and by then all the office staff had left for their home. Parvati too wanted to go, but now since the employer wanted her to stay back, she had to wait, moreover she was indebted to him for employing her.

It was getting late and with no sign's of the guests, she entered his cabin to ask if she could leave for the day. The boss gave her a wicked smile and moved close to her. Parvati could sense the evil intent in his smile. He was wrong about her. Thousands of thoughts flashed through her mind, her two young daughters, the society, villagers, her helplessness, she thought of her late husband, the sudden turn of events in her life, suddenly she felt a firm hand gripping her, holding her tightly. She could not move a bit, he started promising her all the goodies in the world.

What he underestimated was to notice the strength of a helpless lady in despair. Parvati freed herself from his clutch with a sudden force, she picked up the paper cutter lying on the table. Her eyes were raging with anger; it turned red as if she had the power of a thousand suns. She was furious; the initial fear had made way for immense rage. The boss now realized that she was no longer a vulnerable victim, but was now a destroyer in the Durga form. She raced towards him yelling, he could not resist. The next moment he was lying on the floor bleeding from his neck.

The security rushed in, she was handed over to the police.

The case dragged on for a few years, the verdict was in Parvati's favour, the court ruled in her favour claiming that it was an act of self defence. It was Karan who helped her to fight the case. The children were looked after by karan and his wife, who by then had realized that she was wrong in doubting her husband.

On her release, she moved to stay with Karan and his wife, where her daughters were staying.

Here everyone raped a helpless lady, the defence lawyer with his unwarranted questions, media, the society, and the villagers. Her own kith and kin shunned her by cooking up stories about her and spreading them, they defamed her and stripped her of her dignity rather than acting as a support system. The society as a whole let her down.

Life is unpredictable and so is time. Nobody can escape from grief and sorrow, but then bad times are like passing clouds, they come and go, and when they go, the good times return and man has to decide how one chooses to live by. We can choose to curse and cry thinking about bad times or actually think of the little goodies life has bestowed upon us and move forward towards a better tomorrow.

27. Repayment.

Samir was very friendly with all his co-workers working in the mill. Though he was the youngest in the spinning mill, he was very popular due to his helping nature. He respected each and every one in the department.

He was a bright student during his school days, but circumstances forced him to take up this unskilled job hence he was forced to drop out from school.

Rana was also an employee of the spinning department. He was sitting all alone in a corner at the works canteen, looking worried. Samir saw him and headed towards Rana. 'Uncle, what is the matter, you look very much worried and tense! If you don't mind you can share your problem with me'. Hesitantly, Rana opened up; "when you do not find a way out, you hang on to all and everything". He told his financial requirement, if he cannot pay the fees of his son in time, his son will not be permitted to keep his term, he is already late by two months, any time from now, the college authorities will strike out his name.

"Don't worry uncle, you will get the money tomorrow."

Very comforting words, it was a great relief for Rana, who was very much down a few minutes back, smoothing words have magical effects, we see them as miracles or God's blessings.

Time passed, situation changes, the highs and lows in our biorhythm brings good times and bad times; that is the very truth of our life.The good news is; 'Rana's son got employed in the same unit as an HR officer.'

The company was very old. Due to poor maintanance and negligence of the technical staff, the plant condition had gone from bad to worse. With the passing time, it's problems multiplied manyfold. The management was facing lot many problems due to globalization, it was difficult to compete with other players in the market. The experts advised for rightsizing the strength of this old company. They also needed to introduce cost cutting and other necessary steps to strengthen the plant as well as the market trend.

In this present drive they also raked up the old pending charge sheet cases of workers and started fresh enquiry. In one such case, Samir was summoned by the HR department and he got fired from the job. This hard decision was taken by none other than Rana's son.

Samir lost his job, this spread like a wild fire, unbelievable!! The man who was very close to Rana, who helped Rana's son to complete his education, did this to him. Rana contacted Samir and told him "I will talk to my son, how can he do this to you."

Samir was a mature person, "uncle, your son has done nothing wrong, he has done what was conveyed by the management. I will fight my case up to supreme court, do not worry about me."

Rana protested, "he should know, what he is today is only because of you. If he has an atom of love and self respect, he must quit his job other than taking such steps."

"No uncle, don't think on such line, he is a young manager, I am an old employee, he has to come up in life, this emotional hiccup will only pull him down, it should not be a hindrance in his career path."

Samir left the scene leaving Rana in deep thought. Samir had shown the way to life. He had explained what is forgiveness, the joy of giving and conveyed the basic fact never mix professionalism with emotions.

28. Black and white.

Most people around us live in hope. They love life irrespective of what life offers them; is it to be believed they are afraid of death? Probably yes; when we ask them, everyone will say; "we are not afraid of death, sooner or later we have to face them."

One thing is sure, people know what life is; death is unknown to them; naturally we love the known, more than the unknown.

Everyone expects peace during the last phase of their life; people say our life is shaped on the basis of our past karma in our previous birth.

Mohanlal and Vandana's struggle of upbringing their children, to educate them is appreciatable, with his meagre salary.

Mohanlal retired ten years ago, he is now staying with his wife Vandana in their own house independently, but do they have peace of mind?

This old couple is one way happy as they are free from all responsibilities. Their daughter Sanjana is married to an IT Engineer, they live in Hyderabad. Elder son Mitesh is also an Engineer, he is married and stays separately close to his work place. The only worry is about the second son Gaurav, he did not complete his studies, not yet married, he does not have a steady job.

They believe Gaurav is in the bad company of friends, even his elder brother also avoids to meet him or talk to him. He smokes, drinks alcohol and gambles. He says he only does this occassionally, but soon it will run down into the system, then the escape root is very difficult, however, strong a person is. Mohanlal's relatives and friends tried to advice Gaurav, but it was too late, he was beyond that stage of counselling.

His younger sister Sanjana always had a soft corner for him from childhood. Gaurav had a softer side, which probably everyone failed to notice except Sanjana.

Mohanlal never allowed him to enter his house because of his bad habits and other activities. Vandana always felt there is something wrong in the upbringing of Gaurav or they must have failed somewhere in moulding him to be a decent person. She blamed herself for this failure. She hardly had any contact with him except Mohanlal occasionally blurts out whatever information he gets from his circle when he goes to the market.

Mitesh has a decent lifestyle, good friend circle, high contacts and a well-educated wife with two little children. On weekends they visit Mohanlal and Vandana. He too cut short his ties with Gaurav.

The siblings of the same parents brought up in the same house, in the same environment, but totally different in nature. This is the thing which Mohanlal and Vandana failed to understand.

Gaurav never tried to change himself; never bothered what others thought about him. Whenever Sanjana comes home on a short holiday, he makes it a point to meet her, he will shower plenty of gifts on her. She always used to tell him she is not in need of all these gifts, she only wished to see him settled in life. Gaurav never used to visit her home, he knew he is not a welcome guest at their house too.

Gaurav's friends' were from a different background, most of them were more human than the average people. They may be having some personal bad habits, but they never capitalised on someone's weakness, they have never taken advantage of the poor or the weak people. They never tried to cheat to make easy money. Gaurav used to tell, "this is my family". He was free to go to any of his friend's house. Sometimes when lonely, he used to think he had more freedom at his friend's house than his own; now virtually his family disowned him.

It is generally believed that, when your children are grown up, educated, settled in life your responsibilities are over, so one must go for a pilgrimage and pray for peace and harmony for self and others, but does anyone get peace? There are many who say that peace is something we have to find in our inner self, no one can give us peace, some say only death will solve all our problems. The main problem is we are not ready to allow sorrow to go away unless we release sorrow to go away from us, happiness can never enter in to our lives. Mohanlal and Vandana were hoping for peace at the fag end of their life, they had many complaints with life.

One day Sanjana came home suddenly; she was crying unconsolable. Mohanlal and Vandana could not understand what went wrong with her, they tried to find out the reason. Mitesh her elder brother was also summoned. This is the fifth year of Sanjana's marriage. She had problem with her husband all these years. She tried to conceal her sufferings from her parents, it has reached to a level where she cannot take anymore. Mohanlal asked Mitesh to go to Hyderabad and sort out the differences.

Next day Mitesh was to go to Hyderabad, his wife suggested to take Sanjana along with him to Hyderabad, Sanjana refused to go. She said I am ready to die, but I do not wish to go back. I had enough suffering all these years.

On the advice of his wife, Mitesh dropped the idea of going to Hyderabad. Mitesh too kept away from this issue. They knew if Sanjana sits home, she will only be a burden on them later in life.

Mohanlal was helpless. He did not know what action to take. He was completely confused. Two days after Sanjana came home, her husband phoned her to come home immediately, he threatened otherwise he would forcefully take her back. He also warned Mohanlal, if they were not sending Sanjana back he will make rest of their lives miserable. Vandana was worried; she did not know what to say and whom to go for advice. She thought the fault must be Sanjana's; after all she should listen to her husband and take care of her family.

That evening Mohanlal called Sanjana to know the truth of the matter. He was shocked to learn that her husband was gay. Mohanlal lost his mental balance. He wished what she told is all wrong. He was not in a position to disclose this to Vandana. He fainted and was taken to hospital.

Mitesh also rushed to the hospital. Mohanlal was stable. After some time he disclosed the matter to Mitesh. Next day Mohanlal was discharged from the hospital. He reluctantly told everything to Vandana. Their life was firmly in the grip of sorrow and grief. There was no way out, they could only see darkness all around them.

Mitesh's wife also told, "what we can do, Sanjana has to live with it; her husband is ready to take her home; slowly things will be normalised; let us hope things will change slowly but she must go back to her home, when he comes tomorrow , that is the only solution."

Sanjana knew her parents are helpless and old, they cannot take anymore sufferings. She did not wish to be a burden on them. She got all the answers from her sister-in-law. Mohanlal was resting in the next room listening to everything. He was completely drained of all the little energy he had. Mitesh and his wife left for their home.

That entire night Sanjana, her mother and father were all awake; It seemed no end to their agony and sufferings.

Next day morning they called Mitesh to come home as Sanjana's husband was likely to reach anytime now. He said, "I will come there, but the best solution is Sanjana should go back with her husband. With the changing time he will be alright. Sanjana should try to adjust with him, look after her house, you both are very old how long you can support her. I am reaching there as soon as possible."

Sanjana's husband came there with his friend circle in a big station van. He was very rough while talking to Mohanlal. Sanjana was inside the room. He never had the slightest respect for Vandana or Mohanlal. He wanted to see Sanjana, take her along with him. Meanwhile, Mitesh reached there.

Mohanlal started his conversation in a very polite manner. "Sanjana is not ready to come right now, let her stay here for a few more days. She is not in a proper mental frame right now." Sanjana's husband was not in a mood to listen to them. He was over confident in the company of his friends. He said "nothing doing, you cannot confine my wife this way; she will have to come right now, we have come here to take her back." Sanjana came out of the room, she said, "I will not go anywhere with you, not even my dead body." Her husband was furious. He lost his temper, he advanced towards her. Mohanlal came in the middle, he thrashed Mohanlal, took hold of Sanjana. He was about to slap her; just then Gaurav shouted on top of his voice, he held his raised hand, "leave her or else I will finish you here itself." He loosened his grip; Sanjana freed herself. Mitesh was helping Mohanlal to get up and made him sit on an arm chair.

Gaurav, the unworthy useless son was in complete control of the situation, he roared like a lion, "I know everything about you, I have collected each and every details regarding you and your shoddy past, my sister has undergone enough trauma; to hell with you, if I have to kill you for the safety of my sister, I will do that and spend rest of my life in jail."

You go and get married to a man. Before the evil in me raises it's head, before I lose my temper, you better get lost from here.

They left the scene. They were sure they cannot match this guy Gaurav.

Gaurav's friends were welcomed for the first time in their home, Vandana served them biscuits and tea.

Sanjana hugged her brother,who came to rescue her at the right time.

First time in his life Mohanlal realised the worth of this useless son. He never ever considered him a "Khota Sikka."

29. No more Candles.

It was summer time, the train at the harbour terminus was about to leave the station; it was bound for Bombay which is now known as Mumbai.

In the reservation compartment everyone occupied their seats. Relatives who came to see off their dear ones were still waiting for the train to move, they lost no time to repeat their advice. Some people were getting very emotional, children travelling in the train were all happy as the train started moving

The vendors with food items were desperately trying to sell their stuff at the last moment to increase their sales. The platform will again come to life by the arrival of another train. A city railway station never sleeps.

This is a sleeper coach, there are several compartments, and no pantry car is attached. I am taking you back on your watch to the year 1979. Passengers were now settling down, trying to forcefully push their luggage under the seats. There were arguments and counter arguments over keeping the luggage. Passengers travelling with more baggage will naturally put other passengers into great discomfort. It looks like some passengers have hired the entire train.

The Ticket Checker knows there will be certain heated exchange of words among passengers, so he starts checking the tickets without giving attention to their talk. Packing and repacking is a good sight to watch.

This is the second week of August so rarely you find the vacation crowd of families, children and ladies. Most of the passengers are male, very few lady passengers. A group of Naval sea men are also travelling in this coach, 14 of them travelling from Cochin to Bombay, sorry! From Kochi to Mumbai.

Kerala is wet. Chennai is alternate days wet. Andhra is wet and so is Karnataka, but what has railway to do with that!! There are people who consume liquor even in train; they can buy any authority, then why not in a train.

Train was running in the approaching darkness of night, vendors will have a poor response as passengers will have their food brought from home at least in this train. The naval group was busy pouring drinks secretly; like the cats drinking milk by closing the eyes; they think no one is watching them, who bothers!!

The truth of the matter is this evil will definitely raise its head once the excess gets into the system.

The middle berths were lowered; passengers have taken their pillows and spread their sheets, the lights went off, most of them occupied their berths. The train was moving, with the sleeping passengers, halting at stations. Those who slept were sure they don't have to get up as they will reach their destination only next day noon.

There are evil forces travelling with these passengers, those meant to defend the country and the people are all fully or semi drunk; they are not in their senses.

A naval seaman in the darkness of the night climbed on the upper birth which was occupied by a young lady. What prompted him to attempt such a heinous act is unpardonable. He started the drink early in the evening, no one could make out he was heavily drunk, he was maintaining a sober and polite look. The evil in him raised the head. There was a wild cry from the lady sleeping there on the upper birth, it was around 11 in the night. He was sleeping at the opposite lower birth, how come he was here? The malicious intention of this man was clear.

The lady was shouting, this guy also protested to say that he did not do anything. The chain was pulled and the train came to a halt.

The guard and TC joined to enquire into the incident. After the initial inquiry, the train moved again with a promise that they will halt at the station to lodge a complaint. No point in stopping the train at a deserted place.

We are good at demonstrations, but when anyone needs help on the street, or in bus or rail no one comes forward to extend a helping hand. We can avoid such incidents when it happens in front of us, but normally no one bothers. People later on come out with candle light protest.

I supported this lady, no one dared to interfere; it was none of their business. They thought they have to get down at Kalyan or Bombay, why poke their nose in this affair, "it was height of selfishness."

The railway police arrived; they came to our coach with the guard and TC. They made an inquiry and tried to persuade the lady to give up; they cannot possibly take up this case as the train goes zigzags; touching Kerala, Tamilnadu, Andhra; Karnataka, it is difficult to make out where they consumed liquor on a wet day or a dry day, while passing through which state, different states have different rules. Surprisingly these authorities were trying to create confusion, they were trying to avoid their responsibility, they were not focused to the trauma the lady passed through, and it is very unfortunate to see their face saving approach. Their funny explanation shows either they are ignorant of rules or taking the passengers for a ride.

I joined the lady in making a strong point about trying to molest her modesty. The seamen argued there is another dadhiwala (man with beard) pointing to another passenger; who occupied an upper berth next to her.

The lady shouted pointing to the naval seamen, "he was the person who climbed on the berth while I was sleeping."

The railway police finally gave in, they told the lady "we cannot detain the train; you will have to get down to lodge a complaint at this station." He also asked the naval person to get down. He also told the lady to register a complaint with the Railway police office and follow the procedure.

I told the lady; don't worry I will get down with you; provided you are ready for this. She was a very courageous lady; she agreed.

Now the ball was in the opposite court. The 14 naval persons held meeting with the police; they were not ready to get down at the station. The police and the opposition thought the lady will refuse to get down; so they can easily close the complaint without filing an FIR.

They tried to threaten in many ways; but could not do anything as now we were in the full vicinity; the passengers did not support us, but some locals at the station stood beside us.

The train was detained here for almost two and a half hours now, the railway police came with a compromise formula, they said the naval person will apologise to her and don't make an issue as they will lose their job.

They were suppose to board the ship on 14th of August from Bombay port. If they don't make it, they will have to face a departmental inquiry. If the authorities come to know about this incident, they will be court marshalled.

The table turned, we had the upper hand. I left the decision to the lady; she had the lion's heart to pardon him. She hit the man several times with her sandal, all his friends 14 of them were silent spectators.

When we boarded the train after three hours. The co-passengers were all on our side, but not when their support was needed. It was a lucky day for the lady and me, but it will not be the same always, that's why everyone should come forward in extending a helping hand whenever it is required. I told the passengers my wife travels alone during vacation, in the same route, if I do not stand against this now, I will repent forever. "No more candles."

30. D'Souza's.

The year 1954 brought in many changes in our life in many ways. My father shifted from Tata Oil mills Ltd. Palanpur to Tata Chemicals Ltd Mithapur. I was 5 years old. Those days the schooling was very easy since there were no Nursery, LKG or UKG. The first standard admission was strictly on attaining six years, (if we study the date of birth pattern in those days, we will find in most of the cases it will be registered as 1st June-manipulated to get admission). We were luckier than the previous generation and our present generation as far as enjoying our childhood is concerned. We had no botheration of carrying the heavy bag, mugging up the rhymes and the burden of carrying out the home work.

I studied two standards at Mithapur KPS, 3rd and 4th at Kerala in our own school and again joined my parents at mithapur from 5th standard.

So when I joined 1st standard at KPS Mithapur the only language known to me was Malayalam. I had no friends, D'souza's were barely 25 meters from where we stayed.

D'souza's were a great attraction for me. It was as if I was visiting a zoo. A dog, couple of cats, caged birds, hens, milking cows and calf. Our daily milk supply was delivered both times from D'souza's. Eliza their daughter used to come regularly with the milk and my mother will never allow her to go without giving whatever snacks we had in our home. She was like a family member. This was the break she enjoyed to play with me from the busy schedule of helping her mom in the daily chore of house work. Eliza was may be two years elder to me. I never saw her going to a school during that period.

She had a loud dominant voice which was nothing but trying to explain me using mixture of all the words she new from her dictionary with her broken english, hindi and goawanese. In reply, I will react only in Malayalam the language which was difficult to follow.

I have not seen much of uncle who was very old .Aunty used to be always busy with her work of feeding the hens, birds, dog and cats. She was milking the cow herself. Because of all these domestic species, she always gets into verbal arguments with her neighbour, who were vegetarians. The fight reaches to great velocity, but aunty will never give up. The neighbor lady will get inside and close the door. Next day they will be again talking as if everything is normal. The pure milk supply was from D'souza's. The men of both houses will never interfere in the fight. Aunty was so honest, my mother used to say she gives pure milk without adding water.

Eliza was well-trained in all the domestic chores and helps her mother. Whenever I go to her house to play, she will hurriedly finish her work and take permission from her mother to play with me.

After almost a year we lost contact. Eliza was shifted to a boarding school at Bhavnagar. I joined first standard at KPS Mithapur. In those days all the students from standard one to four were accommodated in a make shift room of staff club. It was difficult to differentiate who belonged to which standard except for sister Philomena of St. Ann's church and her helping hand.

We shifted to another area in the township. D'souza's also left for Goa, thus ending a wonderful time of exchanging love, affection, caring and friendship without knowing the language of each other. I have no contact with them after 1955, but the memories will never fade, at least a solace to showcase them in this form.

There are times when we cannot say goodbye to some of our friends and relatives. Maybe that is an indication that we might meet again on this globe. I conclude with a hope that I will meet Eliza some day.

31. A day with an MLA.

The man I was accompanying was an elected MLA. Son of an ordinary postman of a small village sub post office. He was elected on a leading Political party's ticket, no mean achievement!!

Elections in India are like festivals. We see more glitter and glamour during election time. All political parties targets each other, indulge in mudslinging, using foul languages, instigating party workers to arm up against each other, the candidates and parties distribute cash to the voters in backward areas while begging for their votes. Liquors are distributed freely in villages and cities, working on cast equations, gifting saris, household articles, after all we are the largest democratic country in the world.

During the freedom struggle Shri Subhashchandra Bose once mentioned, "every country should adopt dictatorial rule for some years after they get freedom, which will be good for any nation."

Our MLA's basic education was S.S.C. He was looking after several businesses, like construction of roads, operating mines, and farming. He was also very active in politics.

Man gets as per his intelligence is true in his case.

Soon after the elections five of us along with our MLA, travelled in a brand new Ambassador car headed for Ahmedabad, we reached the Party guest house just half an hour before midnight.

The Guest house keeper was not ready to provide us accommodation since we were not having any permission letter from the party secretary. He was not intimated by any of the higher authorities about our arrival. We were also unaware of the procedure to be followed, our MLA also made it for the first time and won the election, so he did not know anyone from the guest house administration. Our elected MLA was also not very comfortable with the city culture, his secretary belonged to the same village of our MLA. In his new avtar (Role) as a secretary his job was to look after the money matters and to remain with the MLA as his shadow, he had no formal education, nor he was supposed to draft letters or deliver speeches, but he was a great manipulator of vote bank politics, prior to the present role he was in the business of selling "Ghee" (Clarified butter).

I was the most educated and youngest among the five, with a Pre university and a second year diploma back ground (in between my studies and vacation). With all my mannerisms and skills I tried to convince the guest house keeper to provide us the accommodation for the night with an assurance that next morning we will get the clearance from the Party officials, as telephones were not very common those days, for making a call one had to go to a post office to make a trunk call. Some offices and certain rich families had the facility of telephone. There were no STD booths, which dominated the scene in the nineties, even that seems to have lost to the mobile revolution of this century.

The Guest house keeper was adamant and not ready to accommodate us. Our repeated pleas and requests went in vain, he was not interested to entertain us without a permission letter.

All along this time our MLA was keeping his cool. He neither protested nor argued like us. Suddenly in the presence of the guest house keeper he asked his secretary to bring the handle bar from the car and instructed him in a stern voice to break open the locks of two rooms ,then turning to us he said ' let us take rest, In the morning we will see what to do.'

On hearing this guest house keeper panicked, after some resistance he gave up, and opened the rooms for us without any fuss.

On the contrary an educated person would have either moved to a hotel or would have waited till morning to get the clearance from the authorities or would go looking for the house of the secretary during that night.

The practical aspect of the problem was getting an immediate attention, the time was different in those days, this is where the leadership of a person counts, the timely action and protection of self and their people.

"Waiting for the next day to lodge a complaint to higher authorities will not solve your present problem", considering the communication facilities available in those day.

It is a great lesson for the modern day Management students," However educated or intelligent we are, only courage and guts to stand against all odds will bring success."

32. The scare crow.

Right from my youthful days till this day at the age of 73, I am projected as a scare crow by parents both known and unknown.

They, while travelling or when they meet me, try to scare their children, who at times are difficult to manage."See police uncle will take you away", and points out towards me to the child, they expect me to further nod and acknowledge their remark in order to make their child behave.

It is a mystery even today, why parents adopt such tricks to calm their children, unwarranted they recruit me, place me in the police cadre which surprises me at times, I ask this question every time when I am projected as a cop, "do I really look like a police or do I have a dangerous look?", does the child understand the role of a police at this tender age or is it a simple conditioning of the tender mind of a child, like we do in case of religion and caste. We have made the Police a terrorizing personality, I also carry the tag of a terrorist, to calm the difficult child.

In my personal life I am very fond of children, however tough and difficult a child; they become very friendly when they land on my lap or in my company.

A child may have a headache, stomach ache, or is unable to express ,will cry; and with out trying to understand their problem we try to calm the child by such means.

"Uncle is a police, he will take you away", it rings in my ear and disturbs me. I try to explain the parents not to scare them by the name of police or by any other name. It is time we understand the police, that they are here to maintain law and order, to help us and not as a scare crow. Please let us not project the police in poor light, then what about the children of police !!

How ever hard I try I am still crucified as a 'Scare crow.'

33. Gandhian thoughts.

He was carrying several books written by Mahatma Gandhji, and was returning back after the visit of Sabarmati Ashram. When we visit such holy place; for a while the atmosphere captivates our feelings and bring in wonderful thoughts associated with freedom struggle and the message conveyed to us by Gandhiji.

While flipping through some pages of a book it reminded and refreshed the lost values and ethics.

He continued in a conversation, "I bought these books for my children, they must know about Gandhiji and how we got independence. How much sacrifices our freedom fighters have made to achieve this, they paid a very heavy price for our independance."

A vendor came with a tea cup. It is nice to have tea while discussing different topics varying from politics to film and sports. One other passenger was running an NGO at Kasaragod, he shared lot of subjects with us, from the farmer's plight to stray cattle's problem.

It is nice to travel through konkan route, amidst scenic beauty, plenty of tunnells, lush green fields , coconut lagoon, crossing the rivers through long bridges. beautiful site of fertile soils black and brown and red soils, lush green beautiful natural scenes feast for the eyes.Those who started from the desert land of Rajasthan enjoying the beauty of different cactus will always cherish the changing beauty of nature and it's people. It passes through beautiful goa and Karwar regions.The looks of people of different regions the tall the strong the tough looking guys and equally good looking beautiful ladies with different features, the colourful smiles of children at schools, play grounds speaks volumes of India's diverse culture, the best education is definitely through travelling.

The site of vendors specialy with food items in the southern part are very mouthwatering.You eat more than yor appetite .

At Mangalore our co passenger from Gandhi Ashram asked for an extension of his journey ticket from Kasaragod to Kannur. His reservation was up to Kasaragod, it would be easy for him if he gets an extention ticket to Kannur as his native village is closer to Kannur.The distance between Kasaragod to Kannur was roughly seventy to eighty kilo meters. Since we were travelling in 3rd AC the difference worked out to Rs.400/- (year 2014) .

"It is only rupees thirty five from Kasaragod to Kannur by local train,why should I pay more, I better get down at Kasaragod and proceed by local train."so he did not extend his ticket and the TC left the coach.

This is a superfast train coming from Bikaner (Rajasthan), we boarded from Ahmedabad, the waste bin was full and over loaded with left over foods and all sort of garbage, we made a complaint so it got cleaned at Kasaragod station.

Other co passengers adviced him, "you need not get down at Kasaragod, there is no stop in between Kasaragod and Kannur, this being a superfast train, once it leaves Kasaragod the very next station is Kannur, in case if some one questions you can always tell them that you could not get down at Kasaragod as you woke up only after the train left Kasaragod."

So my co passenger continued his journey, he got moral support from co passengers. We again got engaged in some discussion. Though he occupied the side birth, for convenience he sat opposite me. Ticket checker got in to our coach from Kasaragod and sat beside me, he allotted the side birth of my co passenger to a new incombant. Luckily ticket checker did not ask for the ticket but casually asked where we are heading for. He also joined in our discussion, the coach was almost empty as several passengers got down at Mangalore and Kasaragod. This Ticket checker too will get down at Kannur.

We kept the TC busy with our questions and doubts. We discussed about the lack of facilities provided by the railways, he too had lot of complaints on duty hours,about general complaints, shortage of staff etc. After some time he moved to next compartment, my friend co passenger was greatly relieved.

After getting down at the next station he wished to gift me a book, which I politely refused as it was meant for his children.

We parted ways after having a cup of tea at the station canteen at Kannur.

After he left streams of questions surfaced in my mind, how difficult it is to speak the truth for even a small matter. How much difficult it is to stick to truth or speak the truth. We are good at advising others in advocating certain qualities at the same time we miserably fail when it comes to practice the same in our life.

"Let us practice what we preach".

34. Brain Drain.

It is a very lengthy name, 'The Parent's association of overseas working children'
This is a local association based at Mumbai, it is possible such associations may also exist in other metros and big cities.

Today there is a meeting at a government high school building followed by a dinner on contributory basis at a nearby restaurant.

I accompanied a friend un-invited to this venue. I was reluctant but he insisted, more over it was a contributory dinner so there will not be any objection to my attending this meeting.

My children are all settled in India, my youngest son got an offer from gulf but he refused the offer, on the grounds that, he will be happy to work here.

I could count roughly fifty members. I asked my friend Deshpande, why only fathers are assembled and not mothers in this meeting?

I was surprised on the exclusion of ladies. Deshpande's answer was equally surprising as he mentioned "it is basically for our convenience to meet each other. We formed this senior citizen's group to meet here and discuss various topics from politics to other issues on daily basis, have tea and snacks to pass our evening time exchanging our thoughts. Ladies will have meetings as per their convenience in their own circle." I restrained myself from asking him why they named it as 'The Parent's association of overseas working children' but kept mum.

One senior citizen stood up and addressed the rest, he mentioned about the contribution of Indians in the development of other nations. It was not in a well organised manner as these senior people who gathered were from different fields and categories. They were all internally discussing their own point of views, on the sidelines of the speech in progress.

I could make out all of them were financially well off as they have their savings as well as getting financial assistance from their overseas children. Most of them were wearing branded dresses and costly sports shoes.

There were nearly ten speakers, my friend Deshpande's speech was very impressive. He said 'we are proud of our children they have achieved greater heights, their contribution to the world is remarkable. Look in every field from technology to medicine our children have played a major role. It is because of our systematic upbringing. We have undergone greater pain physically, mentally and financially to educate them to reach to a level where they are well settled now. Today we can afford all costly electronic gadgets, to keep ourselves updated with the modern technology. We are here to celebrate the achievements of our children.'

I was just listening and enjoying, it was altogether a different experience for me, I thought of my children, why I did not get such proud moment!! After all it is money that counts at the end of the day. I was lost in my own world of thoughts for some time.

One old gentle man got up to speak, my friend Deshpande told me, he is Kulkarni, his two sons are in US, one daughter in UK and another in Germany all married and well settled they are well qualified, holding high positions.

Though old in his eighties, Kulkarni had a very strong voice of a young man, he was the home secretary in Maharashtra government. He said, "I am happy to hear all my colleagues who delivered their opinions, if those opinions are made consciously then its fine, but I differ from all of you."

Kulkarni added with strong voice, "there is something wrong in the upbringing of our children. They are sending us dollars, we are well off financially is not the issue here, they are not ready to work for our country because of the poor working condition and salary. I would be happy if they come back and try to improve the conditions here, they must work to bring greater opportunities for their countrymen, unfortunately they are after wealth and power they are not ready to sacrifice their comfort and luxury for the sake of their countrymen."

"Believe me the fault is with us, in our upbringing that's why they left us here, though they know we need them here with us, they cannot let go the luxury, comfort and money for the sake of their parents and country. We are hypocrites, unable to speak our mind clearly. We have to find out where we have gone wrong!!"

There was pin drop silence after the speech of Kulkarni. I now realise,' I did not fail, when my younger son refused the offer of a gulf job, he said "there is enough opportunities in our country why should I go to a foreign land, I will work for my country."

35. Best friends.

Our Ex-PM Shri.Rajiv Gandhi rightly said, we are lucky during our life if we succeed to find one good friend.

I consider myself lucky to get two greats Dipak kulkarni and Raju Shah. A friendship we maintained for the past 4 decades.Our friendship has weathered many tests, we never had any ego problems with each other.

Dipak Kulkarni is an IIT ian from Powai and Raju Shah B-tech mechanical engineer.

These two guys were different from the other friends I had. They were more lively and lived in the present.

Dipak though an IIT ian was not very much ambitious but was very clever and a thorough professional. He joined Tata Chemicals and served for five years then moved to Mumbai his home town and retired from a Senior position from M/s.Nocil. His wife was first a school teacher and later on worked with State Bank of India Mumbai.

The Kulkarni's lived life with a definite plan, the credit should go to Ranjana bhabhi. Dipak was very professional when it comes to work but in personal life he is not a very ambitious person. He never believed in amassing wealth, he is very sensitive to the problems and issues of masses. He always thought and believed in the human capital and treated every workers with respect, which earned him great popularity among employees working under him.

I have yet to see a parallel of both Raju Shah and his better half Deepa. Both very jovial, friendly with plenty of positives. I have found Raju always smiling and full of life. Raju and Deepa discovered a meaning to life, they can find happiness in what ever they undertake, even the hardships of a difficult journey, or a boring movie they will find enjoyment and derive happiness from it.

It is difficult to match their attitude and approach towards life. They believe in the present, make every moment enjoyable.

Some how we three go well with each other, when we meet we always discuss our past blunders. Once Raju got injured in an accident as auto overturned while coming from a movie, he was kept under observation. Lckily myself and kulkarni escaped from any injury or harm.

Kulkarni was his reliever in the mechanical work shop. Myself and kulkarni visited Raju at the hospital, Raju was sitting on a chair placed beside the bed. Kulkarni got in to the patient's bed and lied down as it was visiting hours for the dependants. Just then our divisional head visited on knowing about this incident. There was not enough time to put back Raju to his place of rest (the patient's bed). After a brief discussion and taking stock of the accident details, the Boss ordered, 'Raju you go in nightshift, Kulkarni you take rest'. We then explained it is Raju who is admitted and not Kulkarni.

Since then every time we meet we laugh over this episode Our boss could not conceal his smile.

Boss could not believe he never expected such things does happen in a very organized world.

We meet occasionally, free ourself from all our schedules and discuss everything under the sun from politics to corruption remembering the olden days, the past, everything comes under the scanner when we get on the rocks, nothing stops there, as now Raju is in command, there is no limit.

They are true friends adds meaning to life and it's philosophy.

36. Tribute to my pet Tommy.

On 26th December 2004 Tsunami hit very badly on coastal Indonesia, Srilanka, Andaman Nicobar islands, Chennai, Cudallur, eastern coast of Kerala and Nagapatanam taking the death toll to unimaginable figures. It was a natural calamity, a disaster suddenly engulfing thousands of lives, leaving thousands homeless.

At Nagapatanam a pet Dog saved the life of a seven year old boy. When the boy was carried away by the tsunami waves, his pet dog jumped in the sea and carried back the boy to shore safely swimming against the current .The boy's mother was so overwhelmed by the act of her pet dog that she publicly acknowledged that she loves her pet just like her son.

Dog's faithfulness is known to everyone. This particular incident reminds me of our pet Tommy. Years back, I was hardly 10 or 11 years old studying in the 5th standard, I had to leave my grandparents at Narakkal (Kerala) to join my parents at Mithapur. Tommy was more restless than me as if he knew his association with me is going to end very soon.

I remember he always used to accompany me to school, market, and play ground even to the river where I used to go for swiming. We used to have meals together, we were inseparable.

Suddenly when the day of my departure was nearing Tommy escaped from home, I was desperately looking for Tommy everywhere, I could not find him nor did he return. Days passed but Tommy did not return and I was very sad, I could not eat or sleep properly. My grandmother told me, because he knew you are going he left the house. But nothing could console me. A distant uncle who came from another village explained to me, "Do you know when a dog feels rabies or other forms of madness coming on him, he escapes from home, and he puts as much distance possible between him and the people he loves, before the biting mania deprives him of the power to distinguish between his master and strangers. Even when he feels death coming on, he tries to crawl away somewhere, to take himself out of the lives of those he loves."

Finally I left our native village and joined my parents but till date I could not forget Tommy that is one of the reasons I discouraged my son to have a pet dog in our house, in spite of his repeated requests.

Very few humans can match the unselfishness of dogs. The dog's adaptability to any environment is very fast and becomes the member of the house in an unbelievably short time. A dog will not eat, except when he is hungry. He will not drink unless he is thirsty.

At times when a male and a female dog are romping together, the barrier breaks down between frolic and anger. The female, in a rage may snap fiercely at the male, were another male to attack him. Thus there will be a furious dog fight. Yet we will see not one of the male dogs will attack a female. Can we humans equal this?

Dogs are good example of normal living and wonderful faithfulness.

37. Invisible eyes.

I am taking you back on your watch, the past always travel with us very much in the present and through future, I wonder is there a future? Yes both psychological and by our watch.

Year 1976 as I told you, you will travel back with me.

It was an old college building with red tiled roofs, partially broken roof tiles, broken window panes shabby walls, earlier it was a canteen room, stands there as a witness to many a celebrations in the past as students used to flock here during breaks. It is still there as a witness to many student elections, but today abandoned by all, just waiting for the time to find a makeover or complete demolition. Who knows what is in store for the future.

Some old records were stored in this room, I went inside in search of those papers, I myself did not know how to go about .The door was opened with a creaky sound, I thought it will come out from the hinges as it was jammed rusty hinges.
It was easy to make out that this room is not opened regularly. Any time the roof could come down. Safety always takes a back seat in India, we are in the habit of risking not only our life but the life of others too, thinking nothing will happen to us.

I could hear flutter and sound of a pigeon desperately trying to come out of this mess, it must have thought of a comfortable stay while entering; but then got trapped in this closed room, must have realised the mistake and now struggling to get it's freedom from this self imposed exile.

This room had no ventilation through which it could escape, the doors were opened rarely. On seeing me, instead of feeling safe it got panicked, it was struggling to get out, flying from one end to the other.

The more I went inside it switched from one end to the other, I tried to help, by keeping the door open, by directing the poor creature towards the door, the pigeon lost its way but then it started shunting from one window to the other frightened as it was resting for a while on the broken frame of the roof tiles, flying again with added vigour to escape from the villain who just entered.

I tried to make room for it to pass through the open door, tried hard to drive out, it got tired and took rest on the edge of a closed window close to the door. I was thinking ways to free the pigeon from here, but all my attempts did not bring any result.

The pigeon must have thought that I am just after its life. The poor creature was scarred of me, I tried various methods to free it, but the pigeon thought otherwise.
Finally I moved away for some time leaving the door open, though I was getting late I allowed myself to wait some more time, finally with tremendous speed it flew out to life and freedom.

In our life too we fail to notice, understand the good deed, help coming from unknown quarters and people. We always look with suspicion, we need invisible eyes to see, experience and recognize the good delivered to us from unknown quarters.

38. Lockdown- In the prison of time.

On a hot lit day in Patna, Ramgopal came out of the prison after serving fifteen long years, for theft and attempt to murder; crimes that he never committed. What an irony, that he was released the day before a nation-wide lockdown was declared.

He is 70 and fragile, sick at the fag end of his life. He headed to join his wife who lives in a small village in Bihar.

Sitadevi, his wife, used to work in an anganwadi and is now retired. She looked older than her age. She somehow managed to repay the housing loans by selling her jewellery and a small piece of land she inherited.

Amidst the probing eyes of the neighbours he knocked the door. His wife let him in, where he occupied the only chair in the room. He looked around to see the pale white walls decorated with nothing but an intricate seam of cobweb.

There was complete silence; probably they were communicating their anger, love, concern silently. Perhaps they've forgotten to express their love over the years of hurtful despair. They were living in the prison of time, living in conflict, in sorrow, in the prison of thought.

She gave him clean towels, soap and a tiny drawer to keep his possessions, which was nothing but a pair of trousers and 2 greyed shirts.

Over a week he tried to make himself at home and helped her in doing little chores around the house.

He observed her closely, although they didn't have much to talk. She managed the house with a pension of Rs 2000 and a BPL ration card.

Time dragged itself almost a month since the lockdown, no sign of an end to this turmoil and travails of grief and pain. Ramgopal assessed, if this continues it will be difficult for his wife to manage the expenses. His sudden entry has disturbed the economy of the house greatly. All his life he has never given her a happy moment. And this was a burden on his conscience. He became restless, as he knew it will be difficult to find a job at this age. Who would give him a job with this background?

He felt a deep pain inside him, he could see only two options in front of him: either he has to leave the house so that she can survive rest of her life with what little she has or end his life altogether.

She could see he was bothered, but she let him be. She did not know if she could offer him help or even console him. He was immersed in deep thoughts all night.

On the next morning she looked for him with a cup of black tea but he wasn't in his chair. She could not find him anywhere.

She ran inside, suddenly she notices a piece of paper sticking out from under the water jar placed on an old rickety table. She picks it up and reads it.

Dear Sita,

It's heavy on my conscience that I have never been able to keep you happy. And I know my coming back has made it difficult for you to manage the house smoothly. In this lockdown, I cannot even try to look for a daily-wage job to support us. Hence I'm leaving. I hope you find it in your heart to forgive me.

Thank you for waiting for me patiently and taking me in without a complaint.

Ramgopal.

Tears rolled out from her swollen eyes, the first sign of any affection for him. If only she said a few words to console him. If only she tried to say a nice word to comfort him.

If only.

39. Trust.

Today while buying essential supplies during the covid-19 curfew relaxation, I overheard fellow shoppers talking about how times were different and trusting people by and large was such a rare thing. This exchange between two strangers triggered a distant memory from my childhood.

On my way back I remembered my mother's words "Trust them they will not cheat" I vividly remember I was in my sixth standard.

It didn't make much sense then, but today I know the meaning of the word 'trust'.

My father had made a kaleidoscope for me and had gifted it to me on my 12th birthday. He had used three mirror strips, pieces of broken glass bangles and transparent plain glass fixed at the bottom and top. While giving it to me, he introduced me to this amazing world of colours and patterns. Each in symmetry to carve out an intricate design. He told me that life is beautiful but one needs to look at it as if looking into a kaleidoscope.

While I was busy exploring my gift, my mother called me, "Thambi, there's a shepherd boy at the door, give him some water" with kaleidoscope in hand I asked her "should I give him water from the tapr?"

It was a hot summer day, ours was the first house on the scenic nariyeli road, the road used to lead us straight to the seashore, and airstrip was on the front side of our home.

Shepherds from adjoining villages used to come into Mithapur in the morning and used to spend the entire day with their animals. They used to return back to their villages before dusk.

The shepherd boy had approached our house as it was the first one on the road. I turned to my mother and asked her again "should I give him tap water?"

My mother said "No, take out some cold water from the matka (earthen pot Refridgerators were introduced very late in India)". Meanwhile amma got a glass from the kitchen. The shepherd boy bent forward with his palms joined together expecting my amma to pour water from the jug, Instead amma served him water in a glass and also offered plenty of badams (a fruit abundantly found across Gujarat) from our compound.

While talking to him, Amma also found out that his father was further ahead on the road somewhere near the seashore. My mother filled a steel water jar and gave it to him to take it to his father. After the boy left with the jar, I asked my mother with a cautionary tone "what if he doesn't return the jug?" My mother replied, "Trust them they won't cheat".

Just before sunset the shepherd boy returned with the steel jar, it was filled with MILK.

Life is short and beautiful, one must look at life as if looking into a kaleidoscope, and things will start looking beautiful.

40. Teacher's day (MHS 1963)

A week before "Teacher's day" in the year 1963, it was decided by the school management that the students themselves will take classes as per their choice; which will bring a change and a difference in the style of celebration of teacher's day.

The school was at that time under the stewardship of Mrs.Wankadia madam and the vice principal was Shri.K.H.Pandya Sahib.

Several students took part in this and gave their names to their respective class teachers. Mostly all bright students, also some notorious students too enrolled themselves to be "Ek din kaa teacher". The bright students opted to take class in the lower classes, so that they can give proper justice to the one day students of the class and this breed of one day teachers were very serious for the task they undertook. Students good at sports opted for PT and sports.

In the year 1963, I was in 8th standard, we were in the old SSC where 11th standard was considered as Matriculation. When most of the students opted for lower classes, I opted to take class for 10thstandard, to this date I do not know why I took such a stand; probably I wanted to be different than others, but the fact of the matter is, I was not in the list of bright students, say I was not good in any subject particularly, which probably surprised many of the teachers (if they recollect) even my friends too thought that I took a bad call.

I opted to take Hindi class for 10th students. After giving the name I knew I made a mistake and wished the programme to be cancelled, or if some teachers remove my name for the good, as I myself had no courage to go and cancel my name. Knowing my dilemma my father encouraged me, my battery got charged but only to get fused when I go to school.

Finally I approached Shri.Sharma Sahib who was our Hindi teacher for guidance. I knew I was not in his good books as I hardly managed to get average marks in Hindi and Sanskrit. Initially I could notice that Sharma sahib was not very happy with my choice, as he told me that; I could have opted to teach in the lower class with some other subject. I stood before him dumb stricken as an idiot.

I was in a dilemma, there is a proverb in Malayalam, "If you catch hold of a tiger's tail, you can neither hold it nor leave it."

Thus started my evening one hour session for 3 days with Sharma sahib , and this taught me the importance to succeed, I was serious for this class , and determined to deliver.

Finally I dressed like a teacher and put on the new pant got stitched by Vaghela tailors on urgent basis and entered the class room of my 2 year senior's. Some seniors were making comments on me, I myself was feeling lucky that I was wearing a full pant as I could feel myself, my legs were shaking / shivering, but I put a brave front and took charge of the class. I did not bother about the comments passed by some section of the students, but thanks to late Illaben Dhruna (who was the sister of my class mate Mahendra), who came to my rescue.

While I was taking the lesson, 2 regular teachers sat there as observers (Nanubhai Sahib and Patel sahib). I was confidently taking the class, the boy who never knew his 8th standard lessons was fielding all the questions asked by the class.

I had tremendous satisfaction and was sure I delivered the best way possible; everything I prepared with the guidance of Sharma sahib.

End of the day several of my seniors appreciated my efforts. When I went to thank Sharma Sahib he told me that he already got the report that, I had conducted the class nicely and he is not going to repeat that topic in the class again.

It was a wonderful experience altogether, which always reminds me whenever I am placed in a difficult situation.

41. Hasmukh.

It was a Saturday, I was busy from morning 8.00 am onwards at the office with some important work, and I did not get up from my seat for almost three and a half hours. Finally around 11.30/45 am I got up, I saw my old friend Hasmukh Takodara approaching me; we used to call Hasmukh as "Hakka". I asked him to sit for a while as I rushed to the wash room, I told him; I will be back within 2 minutes.

I was back immediately but Hasmukh was not there; he already left for his department.

The whole day I was busy with my work, went home late in the evening, next day was Sunday, and as usual the rest day was spent at home.

Hasmukh and myself where classmates from primary 5th standard to 11th STD (Metric), we studied in Guajarati medium. When we were in 6th standard the management started the first batch of 5th standard (Eng.-med) under the high school wing. Both English medium and Guajarati medium was managed by Principal Mrs.Wankadia a great administrator and disciplinarian.

Hasmukh was a great sports person, you name it and he will be there whether cricket, hockey or football. He was also good at table tennis and other indoor games, though he never looked athletic he was an excellent sports person. I must say he was very fond of Ganthia Jalebi.(Ganthia is made from gram flour and Jalebi is a sweet-both famous snack of gujarat.)

He was a non-controversial and peace loving person. I have never found him fighting or arguing with anyone. (Hasmukh is late Shri.Govindbhai Takodara's son and brother of Mohan and late Keshubhai).

Monday morning I reached office as usual only to find that Hasmukh (Hakka) was no more; he passed away in the morning. On hearing this I left for his home to express my condolences to the family.

Later on I found that on Saturday just after visiting my office he headed for the central laboratory, while climbing the laboratory steps he collapsed and was rushed to the hospital. He had a massive heart attack. On Monday early morning on 14th November 1994 he left for heavenly abode.

Even today this incident is weighing heavily on me, disturbing my inner self, probably I was the last person he met before hospitalization, I would have been the last person who must have communicated but I feel sorry neither of us could talk to each other, probably he wanted to say something to me… life is with many ifs and buts. Time is more powerful, "If someone gives us their time; they give part of their life to us".

From that day onwards, when ever given an opportunity to meet a friend, I never avoid or give an excuse, because time is more powerful.

42. Hunger (at the backdrop of Covid 19).

Ramu has been working with a small business firm for the past one year. Following the lockdown declared by the government, his world trembled down altogether, leaving no option but to go back to his village with his wife and a six-month old child. Since all means of transport had ceased, they started by foot with their belongings and the paltry amount his wife had saved for difficult times.

They covered a distance of nearly sixty kilometres in three days in the scorching heat with the hope that things will be alright once they reach home.

He phoned his village neighbour asking for his father to which the neighbour obliged.

"Papa it is me Ramu, how are you both? We decided to come back to the village. I lost my job due to the lockdown; we are nearly starving. We have covered some distance by foot, hoping to reach Delhi in two days' time. We are completely broke and do not know what to do". There was a hissing voice from the other end. Since his father didn't respond but in sighs, he asked to speak to his mother.

"Hello Maa it is me your Ramu"... "Yes my child how are you? You are all in my prayer. I heard everything that you spoke to your Papa.

Since you left last year we are struggling to survive. Your Papa is old and sick and not getting any work. I too have several ailments. We were almost starving to death when a noble soul came to our rescue and arranged for one-time meals for us.

Ramu, there is nothing you can do here, you stay where you are. If you come here the person who helped us might stop the meals thinking that you'll take care of us. Stay safe my child. God bless you."

And the line disconnects

About the Author.

Prior to publishing this book he has written and published short stories, poems and won prizes. Published articles in english on Management issues.

Worked with M/S.Tata Chemicals for 37 long years and retired in the year 2009 after attaining superannuation.

Retained by the Tata Management one year after retirement in 2010.

Worked as Manager Administration with M/S.Jay Chemical Industries Ltd, Khambat (Gujarat), after retiring from Tatas.

He can be reached at : anagh91@gmail.com

www.ingramcontent.com/pod-product-compliance
Ingram Content Group UK Ltd.
Pitfield, Milton Keynes, MK11 3LW, UK
UKHW021647190726
13853UKWH00001B/109

9 789354 724350